DEAD BEGINNINGS

Taniquelle Tulipano

A *Bella Tulip* Book
First published in the United Kingdom by CreateSpace 2015
This edition is published by Bella Tulip Publishing 2016

Cover design © Copyright Arijana Karcic,
Cover It! Designs 2015
Book Cover Image © Copyright Konrad Bak 2015

DEAD BEGINNINGS

Paperback 9780993562600
Kindle 9780993562617
ePub 9780993562624

Editing/Proofreading Rebecca Weeks, Rebecca's editing services

Book formatted by Rebecca's editing services

Bella Tulip Publishing
83 Ducie Street
Manchester
M1 2JQ

http://www.bellatulippublishing.com

For the love of my life, my soul mate.
This is for you G.

PROLOGUE

If you were to tell me a month ago that my life would be where it is now, I would have phoned up the nut house and made a reservation for you A.S.A.P.

I was innocent and gullible, but above all, I was naive. Naive to think that everything was black or white. Right or wrong. Yes or no. Naive to live the life I had, I was trapped, and I just accepted it. I never went looking beyond the horizon, never ventured past the end of my own nose.

How much I would have loved to escape the little bubble I was in but was scared of change and loss. I bound myself up in bubble wrap for protection, yet a mold forced me to be the kind of person I didn't want to be.

Work, eat, sleep, work, eat, sleep. My world was a conveyor belt; every day was the same old tune playing over and over. What I needed to do was to change the track, step up the tempo. One person did just that, they took away the radio and replaced it with a live orchestra. The song was played so beautiful; it was heartbreaking.

It all started on an average day that went on to become anything but ordinary.

CHAPTER ONE

Rosannah

"You're so lucky," Brianna moans. "I would give anything for that job," she says with puppy dog eyes.

"That job was delegated to Rosannah, and I won't let her swap with you," Marie chastises, making us both jump a little. She appears out of nowhere and now saunters back to her office, closing the door behind her. Marie is our manager. She's firm but fair. Like a mother trying to be your best friend. To me, it's a strange combination, as I'd rather keep everything separate from my mother. It's bizarre that Marie won't let us swap because she normally lets us. Maybe she's clamping down on that.

Brianna pulls a face towards Marie's office.

"I really don't understand this fascination with the Monstrum place. It's just a house," I say as Brianna turns to face me again.

"Just a house?" she squeaks as her eyebrows shoot up. "Rosannah, there have been legends and stories that surround that house and its residents," she says excitedly. Then her expression turns serious. "They're rumoured to be vampires," she says with awe and wonder.

I can't hold my amusement in and burst out laughing. "Don't be so ridiculous. Vampires don't exist," I manage to get out between giggles. Brianna has a wild and vivid imagination. She can conjure up the most bizarre stories for my amusement at the drop of a hat. I have to hand it to her; she has talent.

"It's true; no one has ever been allowed in or near that house. And the people who live there? They never age. This is the first time they have allowed any outsider into the house, and you get to go. You don't even know who they are!" she says throwing her arms up in the air.

They're the Monstrums, right?

"Tell me everything when you get back, please, please, please, please," she begs.

What else would I do? This girl is just pure drama. "Of course, as long as you shut up," I say with a giggle. Brianna shoots me a wry smile. "I will have nothing but normal things to report back to you," I tell her as I look at the clock. It's two thirty, and I need to get going. I'm meant to be at the Monstrum place at three fifteen, but I want to be a little early to take a good look around the front of the house.

I hop into my gorgeous Anthea. She's my Fiesta Ghia in Panther Black, a gift from my mum. I strap myself in and turn on the radio. "Lullaby" by The Cure blasts out at me. I love this song. I try to deafen myself with my own singing as I pull away. My thoughts soon turn to the Monstrum place and its residents. I wonder what they look like. Cloaks, fangs, coffins? Maybe I should stop off and get some garlic on the way. What the hell am I thinking? Brianna and her bloody stories. It's probably some old boy who's nearly pushing up daisies. I cringe at the choice of my words. His name is Mr. Raphael Monstrum. Be a bit more respectful! I scold myself.

Thirty-five minutes later, the radio is off, and the sat nav is giving me directions.

"Turn left onto Sycamore Lane," it states.

That's the road where the house is situated on, and it cuts through a huge field. The right side is pasture dotted with cows and sheep, and tall conifers line the other side. They're so close together that they cast me into the shadow, like a temporary night. "I bet those trees could tell a few stories if they could talk," I think aloud.

There are two breaks in the trees up ahead.

"You have reached your destination," the sat nav says when I reach the first break.

I pull in and set back from the road is an enormous wrought iron gate. Two large white stone columns, each crowned with a huge lantern, anchor each end. They have no bulbs in them, and the glass panels are either missing or broken. The column on the left has a plaque that says 'qui possit ingredi non potest exire' "What the hell does that mean?" I exclaim to myself. "Looks like Latin at a guess," I answer.

The gates themselves resemble prison bars with the exception of 'VS' encircled in the middle of each gate. "VS? I thought they were Monstrums. Strange," I say to myself. I look around for a buzzer, but there doesn't seem to be one. Just as I'm about to get out of the comfort of Anthea, the gates open. "Hmm, definitely strange," I whisper.

I make my way down a road that snakes its way up to the house. The garden is vast and adorned with beautiful flower patches touched by all the colours of the rainbow. There are also little water features, too, with cherubs and birds frozen in time by beautifully carved white marble.

When I approach the house, there are no cars outside. They must park in the attached garage on the left side of the house. I park on the right, so I'm out of the way. I get out of Anthea and lock her. Crash. I hear a sound in the distance that echoes through the garden and can see that the gates have closed. From here, you can barely see the outside world. It's like you're shut off, cut out of society. A chill shoots down my spine at the thought.

I turn my attention to the house and take it all in. The first thing that I notice is that it's purple. Very, very dark purple. Which is a huge contrast to the clear blue sky that the sun is blazing in. This house seriously looks like it should have a moat, a dragon, and horrible weather. It's a large gothic style dressed in very dark purple stained wood planks. It's two-story and has plenty of window space. The very wide windows decorate the front of the house with dark purple sections and many tiny panels of glass. The house has an open veranda and the steps creak and groan in protest beneath my feet as I walk on them. I go up to a window and peek in. I think I see someone, but in the blink of an eye, whoever it was has disappeared. It must have been my imagination. Double damn Brianna and her crazy stories.

I wander over to the front door, which is also that dark purple. It's large, almost the width of two normal doors, and towers over me. It has four long rectangular panels on it, all intricately carved. A huge knocker hangs in the middle, and it too bears the encircled 'VS' symbol. I reach forward and lift the knocker. It's heavy and crashes back down. Damn it. The noise is thunder around me, vibrating through my body. I pull my hand back as if it has electrocuted me.

Within seconds, the door makes a few clicks and clacks and opens to reveal the most gorgeous man I have ever seen. The first thing that strikes me is his eyes. He has the most wonderful light grey eyes. I've never seen any that colour before. As strange as they are, they have such depth and beauty to them. They shine with intelligence and knowledge. They are eyes that are way beyond their years, set into a face too young to house them. Luscious black hair that goes down beyond his shoulders frames his chiseled face. It has a slight wave and glimmers in the artificial light of the entrance hall. It's almost enough to make me jealous. His lips are full and very pink while his skin is very smooth and incredibly pale. Almost transparent, it's that pale.

My eyes involuntarily skim down his body. He's dressed in very dark blue jeans, an open-collar black shirt, and a full-length black leather jacket. Well, if he always dresses like that, it's no wonder there are rumours about this place! It's a wonderful sunny day, and he has a leather jacket on! He's quite tall, must be at least six-foot-two. He has broad shoulders, and something tells me that he's probably quite toned under those clothes. He emits power and strength even though he looks about twenty-six. I realise then that I'm just standing there staring at him, mouth open. I'm almost catching flies, just to make it more embarrassing. I feel my cheeks heat slightly as I flash a quick, nervous smile.

I clear my throat and hold out my right hand. "Rosannah Morgan from Tilberry Sales," I say just a tad louder than I had intended. I wince slightly and just look at him. He gauges me for a small while, and it begins to get a little awkward. Just as I'm about to pull my hand back, he reaches out and grabs it. As his skin touches mine, my hand tingles, and I draw in a deep breath. His hand is large and fits snugly around mine. His grip is firm, and his smooth hand is cold. It must feel cold because I'm flushed with embarrassment and that thought makes my cheeks flush a little more.

His lips start to move, and my eyes dart to them. "Raphael Monstrum, please come in," he says in a deep, melodic voice. Raphael Monstrum, Junior, right? Raphael Monstrum, Senior, must be inside. Probably on his deathbed. Rosannah! Mr. Monstrum looks down at our hands and lets out a little laugh. I don't understand. He then yanks his hand out of mine. Oh no. I had gripped his hand and hadn't let go! How much more am I going to embarrass myself? He walks off down the hallway, and my hand, which is still held out, suddenly aches from loneliness. How can a hand ache from that? I snap out of my daze and enter the house.

Right, it looks like I'm left to shut the door. Mr. Monstrum may be incredibly good looking, but his manners suck. I attempt to shut the door. It's so heavy that I can't budge it. Mr. Monstrum has disappeared into a room on the far left, and there's no way I'm going to call him, so I put my back to the door and begin to push. Scrunching up my face, I put my all into it and only manage to move it a tiny bit. When I open my eyes, I'm faced with Mr. Monstrum, who's standing there watching me with a slight smirk. The sight of him startles me, and I jump with a yelp.

"I am terribly sorry about that. How rude of me. Here," he says, trying not to laugh, making his way over to me. He uses the back of his right hand to move me out of the way, which causes my heart to flutter. I could have sworn that his eyes darkened a little. He then pushes the door shut with his left hand, ending up extremely close to me. The hairs stand up on the back of my neck as he looks down at me. I've never been this close to a man, and I'm reeling from it. Taking quick shallow breaths, I realise that I can't feel him breathing on me. I look at his chest, which doesn't appear to be moving. Strange. I look back up at him and frown. He smiles, half apologetic, half regret.

"Follow me," he says as he takes a step back and then walks off to the same room he had entered a few minutes before. I quickly follow him in a daze. My mind is still wrapped around how heavy that door was. How did he manage to shut it with one hand and with such ease? Now, I'm no muscle woman, but I'm not a weed, either. That door was extremely heavy; I know it was. Also, what's the whole thing with him appearing not to breathe? Maybe I was too caught up and imagined that bit. As we enter the room, he turns to face me.

"Would you like anything to drink?" he asks.

I look at the distance between us and notice that he's slightly too far away from me. If I keep analysing everything, I won't get my job done! I chastise myself. I let my thoughts go and turn my work brain on. "No thank you, Mr. Monstrum." I smile.

"Please, call me Raphael. Take a seat." He gestures around the room. It's the dining room. The large oak table and dining chairs are a dead giveaway. The room is large enough to have wider dining type chairs lining the walls on either side. I go over to the right one and sit down at the far end of it. The chair is long enough to sit five people on it, but when Raphael sits down, he leaves a two-person gap between us. Maybe he thought to be so close to me earlier was inappropriate or worse, maybe he thinks I'm some crazy bunny boiler because I wouldn't let go of his hand! I look at the gap and then at him. I'm not going to bite you; according to Brianna, I should be worried about you biting me! I shake the thought from my head and dig the paperwork and a pen out of my bag.

"I need to sign something?" Raphael queries.

"Oh no, I just fill this out as I find out certain information about the house. Just a questionnaire, really." I shrug trying not to portray my embarrassment. Thinking about a sickly old man in a bed somewhere in this house, I feel horrid about having to disturb him. Disappointed, too, that I won't be spending more time with this Raphael. "So, who does the house belong to? I have questions to ask the homeowner," I start.

"This is my house," he says.

My eyes nearly pop out of my head. I can't hide my shock. He smiles, clearly amused by my reaction. How could this be his house? He's way too young to own a house like this. "Okay. Erm, how old is the house? Roughly," I ask thrown by this thought.

"Three hundred and thirty-two years old," he says as he stares at me. I start to feel a bit self-conscious and escape eye contact by writing his answers down. I can still see him in my periphery, though, and could almost swear he was staring at my neck. When I look back up at him, his eyes dart up to mine.

"That's quite precise." I flash a quick smile, trying to hide my discomfort. He just smiles; he's obviously quite amused. Again. I clear my throat and get back to my questions. "How many people have owned the house?" I ask.

"It's been owned only by family, being passed down through generations." He smiles wryly, something playing behind his eyes. I look at the questionnaire, there are plenty of more questions, but I can't sit here any longer squirming under his intense stare.

Quickly folding the paper, I put it and the pen back in my bag. Raphael lets out a quiet chuckle, and I can't help but glare a little at him. He bites his bottom lip to stifle his laugh, bringing my attention back to that luscious mouth, and my face burns. Feeling increasingly uncomfortable, I jump up. "Okay, can I take a look around?" I ask as I turn to face him.

"Certainly. This is the dining room." He gestures around the room with his eyes still trained on mine. I'm thankful that his eyes don't flick down my body as I stand here in front of him. I turn and look at the room some more. Pale gold-embossed paper decorates the walls. The carpet is thick, plush, and deep red, reminiscent to the colour of blood. The curtains and the chair covers are plain velvet, also dark red. All the wood furnishings in the room are a shiny varnished oak.

The room is fairly large but quite bland. There are no ornaments or decorations except the exquisite chandelier hanging from the centre of the ceiling. I suck in a deep breath and turn back to Raphael. He smiles at me, gets up, and walks back out into the hallway without a word. I can't help but watch him as he leaves the room. He moves with the utmost grace. I take another deep breath and follow him. He's facing the front door with his hands behind his back. When I reach him, he pivots to face me.

"We shall start at the front and work our way back." He smiles. "Then, we shall go...upstairs." Although it is only a tiny bit, his smile seemed darker when he said 'upstairs'.

He then proceeded to show me all around the house. We passed larger than average magnificently carved oak door and doorways. Silk decorated each room in deep, rich colours, such as purple, green, red, gold, and blue—except for one room, which I dubbed the Dracula room. Raphael didn't keep me in that room long enough to take much in, apart from the fact that everything was black. It must have been a very special room, although, by the smell of the cologne, I assumed it was his room. When I was close to him by the front door, I was too dazed to pay attention to his scent, and now I can't help but wonder what he smells like.

All the curtains in the house were floor length and velvet, held back with matching coloured tassels and no net curtains. I don't understand why someone wouldn't have net curtains. Not having them is like saying, 'Hi there, I may not know you, but here's my personal private space, why don't you have a good look?' But here, I suppose there's no need with all the evergreen trees standing guard around the house.

Dark purple wallpaper with a pattern of almost black flowers clad the walls in both the upstairs and downstairs hallways. It was the background for a showcase of painted family portraits. As beautifully painted as they were, it was strange that they only had first names on the plaques beneath them. No dates that would have marked their lives or surnames were there.

Only two bore any resemblance to Raphael. One exquisite woman with pinned-up black hair and similar eyes, mouth, and nose to Raphael looked out at me melancholy. Her attire was extremely outdated. Period paintings? Why not, there are period style photographs that one can get. 'Our dearest Elizabeth' according to the plaque. The other showed quite a stern and steely dark-haired man, with the only similarity being Raphael's face shape. Same period clothing as Elizabeth. 'Our brave William' was what that plaque stated. So, no Raphael, Senior. Even though I could see they were probably Raphael's parents, they didn't share his eye colour. Elizabeth had ocean blue eyes while William had chocolate brown ones. Where the hell did Raphael's light grey ones come from? Maybe an uncle? Come to think of it, none of the paintings had his eye colour. So maybe not, ah, who cares.

All the floors and the grand staircase in the house were also oak. The staircase was the main focal point of the entrance hall, with two large banisters at the bottom magnificently carved with two flying angels. They looked so life-like, as if ready to take off for flight. The staircase met a circle hallway that bordered the top of the entrance hall. Above the circle hallway was an enormous chandelier hanging from the middle of a smooth domed ceiling. Like diamonds hanging in the middle of a dark halo. The upstairs and some of the bedrooms extended over the garage to make the house a cuboid shape. Along the left of the upstairs hallway were a delightful and charming music room and two bedrooms. One blue complete with en suite and the other was the Dracula room.

Along the back of the house, there were two bedrooms, one red, one purple, also with en suites and a grand bathroom. Along the other side of the house were a further two bedrooms, one gold, one green, and an office. Downstairs on the left was a study and the plain dining room separated by the entrance to the grand staircase. On the right side, there was a TV room and a large hall for entertaining a large number of guests. And at the back of the house was an extremely large kitchen. All the rooms were so beautifully decorated except for the dining room. It was very plain in comparison and the only room that had carpet in it. Once Raphael had finished showing me the house, we went to sit back in the dining room.

One question has been bugging me since I first saw it. I look at Raphael slightly puzzled.

"Yes?" he murmurs, still keeping quite a distance from me.

"I have just been wondering, since I got here, why the gates and door knocker have VS on them instead of an M?" I ask. He laces his fingers together, looks down, and chuckles. It almost looks like he's going to start praying. He looks frozen, like a statue, like he isn't breathing—again. I can't help myself from leaning very slowly towards him, and I try to smell him subtly, but he unexpectedly looks straight up at me. I jump a little and freeze. It's like he knows what I was trying to do.

"It stands for Von Smit. Not all my ancestors were Monstrums," he says emotionless, but I can see the humour in his eyes.

"Oh, I didn't think of that," I mumble, feeling incredibly stupid, and reluctantly lean back up. I need to get out of here, so I get up, intending to leave with my tail between my legs. This has definitely been a strange experience and one that I'm not likely to forget. "I'll be off then." I smile, leaving the dining room—destination front door, quick march. Please follow me and let me out of here.

"What? No valuation?" he queries from behind me.

Damn it. I turn to see him catching up to me with his gallant strides, and I frown. "Oh, even though they've taken off my training wheels and let me come here on my own, I'm still a trainee, and my boss prefers to oversee that part. If I were to tell you the wrong value, the company could be liable," I say reluctantly, a smile trying to hide my horror and embarrassment. Something tells me that he already knew. He walks around me and opens the door with great ease. I eye him suspiciously.

"So, I will hear from you again?" he asks with a raised eyebrow, ignoring my expression and moving to the side so I can leave.

"No, you will hear from Marie, my boss. Anyway, it was lovely to meet you, Raphael. You have a lovely house." I hold my hand back out again, and he grabs it while holding my eyes with his gaze. I feel that tingle again. His hand is still cold, causing me to pull mine away. Maybe he has bad blood circulation or something. This man is strange, and I just want to skedaddle. A frown quickly flashes across his face, and I get that ache in my hand again.

I force a smile, turn around, and hurriedly make my way to my car, without risking a glance back at him. I hear the door close behind me, and I quickly put the back of my hand to my face to see if my cheeks are still heated, but they're not.

I jump in Anthea and the radio blasts out "Strange Condition" by Pete Yorn when I turn her on. I reverse over to the garage and look at the study window. I see Raphael standing there looking me. Oh, God. I glance away for a second, and when I look back up, he's gone. I don't know if I'm seeing things or not, but I need to get out of here. I race back off towards work. While the song is playing, my attention turns back to Raphael and his suspected bad blood circulation. Maybe he's sick, and that's why he's having the house valued. That would explain a few things; the pale skin, the cold hands, the barely breathing, and why he kept a distance between us. But if he's that sick, how did he have the energy to shut that door? He certainly didn't move around like he was sick. I'm just confused. I was very tempted to ask him why he was getting the house valued, but Marie had warned me against straying from the questionnaire when I first joined Tilberry Sales.

CHAPTER TWO

Rosannah

I park around the corner so I can fill in the rest of the questionnaire. When I get back into work, I walk past an extremely excited Brianna and straight into Marie's office.

"Ah, thank you, Rosannah. Please close the door behind you when you leave. I have some calls to make." She smiles as I hand her Raphael's paperwork. Closing the door behind me, I brace myself for Brianna. She pounces on me before I can even sit down.

"Tell me everything," she squawks at me.

"All right, all right. Calm down," I say trying to get her to sit.

"You should have seen her when you pulled up it was like she was sitting on a vibrator," Paul pipes up. Paul is our newest trainee; he's also the youngest at just seventeen. You'd think he'd be a shy timid little mouse, but not this one. Brianna and I shoot him unimpressed glares.

"There was a moment there when I thought she was gonna..."

"That's enough," Brianna cuts him off through gritted teeth. "We're off to a late lunch; tell Marie," Brianna fires at him and drags me out of the office before Paul can say another word.

We only walk a few yards to a small cafe. Tilberry Sales is snuggled in the middle of a parade of shops. Tilberry Parade to be precise, situated on Tilberry

Common. There's a charity shop, a newsagent, our place, a Tesco Express, and Tilberry cafe. Brianna leads me to the cafe and sits me down at a table near the back. Mike, the cafe owner, wanders over.

"The usual, girls?" He smiles a gappy grin at us, appearing not to have noticed Brianna's behaviour.

"Yes, please." I smile at him thankfully.

"Coming right up," he replies as he wanders back into the kitchen. We come here so often and have the same thing every time. It's pretty sad. A mushroom and onion omelette with salad and a Coke for me, and a BLT and coffee for Brianna.

"So?" Brianna prompts me, and I let everything overflow into her eager ears. I tell her everything, but I seem to stick to the topic of Raphael more.

"You are pretty stuck on this Raphael; he's all you've spoken about. How good looking is this guy?" she asks.

"Brianna, he is the most handsome man I have ever seen," I swoon.

"He can't be." Brianna laughs.

"I can only tell you this; he has a face that would make angels weep. Cupid certainly doesn't need to follow him around. I bet he's broken so many hearts. He's a bachelor, who owns a huge house, is stinking rich, and to top it all off, he looks like he's seriously hot under his clothes," I say in a daydream.

"You wouldn't have any idea of what a hot body looks like," Brianna scolds me.

"Okay, so I haven't seen one in the flesh, but you've shown me plenty of pictures," I say lifting my chin defiantly.

"All right, I'll give you that one," she says narrowing her eyes at me.

Brianna agrees that Raphael and his house are weird, but of course, this only fuels her imagination.

"See, he's a vampire," she claims out loud. Her outburst has everyone, including Mike, staring at us. I shoot them all a quick apologetic smile then scowl at Brianna.

"What the heck is wrong with you? Keep your voice down," I whisper.

"All that pale skin and ice-cold hands? He's definitely a vampire," she says crossing her arms.

"Brianna, he could just be really ill!" I chastise her.

"Not with the strength to shut that door. So, if you're sure he's not a vampire and he's that fit, why don't you ask him out?" she asks with a sly smile. She knows that there's no way I'd do it. I've never asked anyone out, and I don't intend to, either.

"Brianna, not only do I not want to go back, but there's no reason for me to go. He just wanted an evaluation, which is in Marie's hands now. Besides, he would just think I was after his money and his house," I say hoping to put this to rest. A small part of me does really want to gaze once again on that masterpiece that is Raphael's face and have the courage to ask him out. But I know I won't be going back, and I'd be too scared to do it, even if I did.

"Well, if he dies, you might get a mention in his will if you play your cards right" She grins. I don't believe her! I glare at her.

"He sounds like he liked what he saw, though," Brianna says pulling me back from my thoughts.

"I doubt it; he can have his pick of any girl. Trust me." I shrug.

"But all that staring," she says raising her eyebrows.

"Brianna, I've never felt so awkward in my life. I could feel his eyes on me," I whisper, embarrassed.

"Eyeing up a tasty meal." She laughs.

"Not even remotely funny," I scathe at her. She just carries on laughing. We finish up and pay the bill.

"Take care, ladies." Mike smiles at us, but I can see the judgement in his eyes.

"Bye, Mike." I just about manage to get out with a half-smile. Brianna is still laughing, causing us more odd looks as we leave the cafe. When we walk back into the office, Paul is smirking. He's up to something. Marie walks out of her office.

"Late lunch?" she inquires.

"Yes, we needed a little getaway," Brianna says throwing a look at Paul. Marie gives us a knowing look.

"Didn't he tell you that we were out to lunch?" I ask. Paul smirks even more, and Marie shakes her head. Little rat!

"Well, Rosannah, it looks like you will need to head back to the Monstrum House tomorrow," Marie says, and Brianna half snorts, half squeals.

"Bless you," says Marie, and I hold back a laugh. I can see the glee on Brianna's face as Marie continues.

"Mr. Monstrum forgot to show you the garage and grounds, and he's insisted that you go back to view it tomorrow morning," she finishes. Oh, no. My head was in such a mess earlier that I forgot about them, too. "Because there's not much for you two to do today, you may as well go home early. You've both worked pretty hard lately." Marie sighs and disappears back into her office. Paul scowls at us. He obviously wanted to get us into trouble. His devious little plan backfired. If he had paid any attention in the three months he's been here, he would have realised how well Brianna and I get on with Marie.

"See you tomorrow," Brianna chimes at Paul. That will teach him! We shut down our PCs, gather our stuff, and almost skip out of the office. Brianna hops in Anthea. She always gets a ride with me because we live in the same apartment block. It takes five minutes to get home, but it is five minutes of pure hell. I have to listen to a barrage of nonsense from Brianna. She's convinced that Raphael has deliberately planned to get me back to his house and that I should ask him out, as it would be so cool if my first boyfriend were a vampire. Although it's funny, on a serious note I'm beginning to wonder about her sanity. She continues her assault as we climb the steps to her apartment.

She lives with her mum and little brother. I secretly thank little Cody when he pulls Brianna away to their flat. His eagerness to play with his big sister saves me. My apartment is on the next floor. Marmalade greets me with a loud meow, doing a figure of eight around my feet while rubbing her side against me. She's a silver Egyptian Mau. She's quite a special breed, according to my mum.

"All right, all right, let me get myself sorted before you trip me up," I tell her while trying to keep my balance. I manage to take my shoes off, hang my coat up, and put my bag away while doing acrobatics about Marmalade. I go to the kitchen and sort her food out because she doesn't bother me when she's eating. I go to the phone and listen to my messages. I hit play and get the usual message.

"It's your mother, call me as soon as you get this." I get the same message every day. It isn't because I can't be bothered to call my mum or even because I need reminding that she exists, it's because my mum is a complete pain in the butt. Don't get me wrong, I love my mum, but she's hard work. I ignore the feeling of dread that has settled in my stomach and call her for the same old conversation that we have literally every day.

"Rosannah," my mum answers the phone in a clipped tone. I have to fight the urge to reply 'no, it's the devil; it's time to pay up.'

"Hi Mum, how are you?" I ask knowing that she won't answer the question.

"Have you got a man yet?" she practically demands.

"No, Mum, the situation is the same as yesterday," and the day before that and the day before that and guess what? The same as the day before that.

"I honestly don't think you try hard enough. You should show them a little of what's on display." She's like a parrot, high pitched and always repeating herself.

"I've said before, Mum, I like subtlety," I sigh.

"Well, it clearly isn't working for you. How's the cat?" she asks.

"Marmalade is fine," I tell her. My mum won't say her name. It goes back to when I moved into my flat. My mum had lots of money and bought me the flat, as she wanted me to be independent. I had begged her for weeks before I moved in to let me have a roommate, as I didn't wish to live on my own. She flatly refused, citing that it would ruin any chances of me getting a man. And so, on my moving in day, she disappeared and then turned up at my flat that evening with a cat, Marmalade.

Marmalade was her excuse as to why she couldn't help me move in. I didn't want a cat, and for weeks, although I looked after her, Marmalade went without a name. My mum badgered me every day to name her. So one day, in pure frustration, I named her after the first thing I saw. I had a jar of marmalade in my hand that my right arm was threatening to lob across the room as my mum continued to wind me up. So, rather than her be happy my cat had a name, she said it was completely stupid. She now doesn't acknowledge it and just refers to her as 'the cat.' I grew to love Marmalade, and we both love her name. My mum then finishes our phone conversation the way she always does.

"I'm too busy to see you at the moment but get out there and find a man. I want you married, and I want grandchildren. If you need anything, call me. Goodbye, Rosannah," and she hung up. Yep, that's my communication with my mum. The exact same conversation, every day. I could phone her out of the blue, too, if I wanted, but I'd get the Spanish inquisition. I also get the occasional gifts sent to me as she likes me to have designer things, but that's as far as my relationship goes with my mother. I then sort my dinner out, snuggle on the couch for a bit with Marmalade, watch junk TV, and then go to bed for much-needed sleep.

CHAPTER THREE

Raphael

"Really, Evangeline, you're beginning to sound like an old, dying record," I say with as much boredom as I can muster up.

"Raph, I just don't understand why you have to have the house valued. It's not like you're dying anytime soon," Evangeline whines for the fifth time. She has a point, but I can't explain that selfishness inside of me that will stop at nothing to get what I want. And what I want is that fine beauty. Eyes as green as the Nile. Hair as dark and rich as chocolate. With the body of a goddess and the voice of an angel, she truly is a masterpiece. How I would love to break her under my iron whip. Let her bask in the glory of my rugged good looks before I reveal my true nature. I will drink her fear and swallow her dreams only to make her forget we ever met. She will be a river of pleasure that I can drink from whenever I please and yet have no idea I ever had a taste.

I only happened upon her by pure fluke. I had been on my way to visit that wretched creature, Harry. It takes less than a few minutes to get to him and the hovel he calls home. Moving as fast as I could, places and faces blurred past me, yet amongst a whirl of noise, one voice stood out. A nightingale almost drowned out by the senseless nattering of nobodies. I have made the route to Harry countless times before, but this was the first time I had heard her voice, and I felt compelled to find her. I followed the voice to the source to see the back of two women immersed in idle chitchat.

The one on the left was dressed in a black dress while the one on the right was dressed in pastel candy colours. I could smell her from where I stood. She smelt like sugar, coconut, and very sweet alcohol. Perfume is a wonderful thing, but it also stinks of alcohol. I then turned my attention back to the boar and gazelle. The left one looked like a sack of potatoes, short and stubby. She had horrendous lumps and bumps protruding in a hideous fashion compared to the one on the right. Elongated, lean, and graceful. The one on the right had amazing proportions and curves in all the right places.

I kept myself out of the way, aware of everyone around me. Most people just walked past me, skimming my shoulder with theirs, as they were more concerned with texting than watching where they were going. I observed the two women as they carried on their conversation. Fully animated like puppets on strings. I paid no attention to what they were saying. Whatever it was, it had them giggling and squealing like children. I was too eager to see her face to bother with their words. Then suddenly she stopped and the boar took a couple of steps before she turned to see what the matter was. Yep, she was definitely a sack of potatoes. Pastel Candy girl threw her arms up in exasperation.

With a twirl, she revealed her face, which was more exquisite and perfectly shaped than I could have ever imagined. She was the most beautiful creature I had ever seen—beauty that only fed my wicked mind. Her face scrunched up in irritation, and she started to walk at a quick step in the direction she had come from. She ducked into a little cafe. Sack of potatoes checked her watch and walked on and into an estate agents rather than wait for Pastel Candy girl. After a couple of minutes, Pastel Candy girl emerged, a handbag in tow, and went into the estate agents, too. I dashed off to Harry's but looked into the estate agents as I passed to see that Pastel Candy girl worked there. It looked like I was getting my house valued.

On my way back from Harry's, I dropped into the estate agents, but Pastel Candy girl was gone. The boss, Marie, was more than helpful. I learnt that Pastel Candy girl's name was Rosannah. A beautiful name for a beautiful girl.

"Raph, Raph. Are you listening to me?" Evangeline says irritated. I snap out of my daydream.

"You are still going on?" I ask incredulously.

"You're up to something. You're up to your old tricks," she says crossing her arms.

"Am I a magician?" I ask deadpan as I begin to push her towards the front door.

"Might as well be, you're too good at making things disappear," Evangeline spits at me. I open the front door and push her outside.

"Fine, but I'm borrowing the Porsche and the two Mercedes," she yells as I close the door on her. A small price to pay. I do not want any of my family here when Pastel Candy girl turns up. I want her all to myself.

I hear Candy Pastel girl's car from down the road. I wait until she has reached the gate to open it for her and watch as she drives down the drive and parks. She gets out and inspects the house. Well, the house is pretty impressive. It's quite large and a striking colour. A dark, deep purple. My grandfather's colour scheme. The steps to the veranda creak as she walks up them, and I delight in the sound.

She then does something I had not expected; she comes up to the window of the room I am in and stares right in. I do not want to be caught staring at her so I race off to the front door. I listen as she moves over to the door and knocks. I brace myself and open the door to see her gawping at me. I watch as she takes my appearance in. Awestruck, she just stands there staring at me for some time. At one point, I thought she might even reach out and touch me to see if I was real. Oh, I am real all right. As true as the sun burns brightly on a summer's day.

I watch as her cheeks flush, mouth open wide. I would have laughed, but I wanted that reaction. I wanted her stunned by my looks. I have wanted females attracted to me, but none of them besotted, with the exception of Rosannah and Emily. But Emily was long gone, dust and bones in the ground. That was all the worms and bugs had left of her. Now she was just a flicker of a few broken memories tucked deep within my mind. But Rosannah, she's all flesh and blood right before my very eyes. She finally comes to her senses and holds a hand out to me.

"Rosannah Morgan from Tilberry Sales," she says with a nervous undertone. I do not want to touch her yet, but she leaves her hand waiting. It starts to get awkward so I reach out and take her warm, soft, pliable hand in mine. She takes a deep breath and her cheeks flush further. Amongst the warmth, I feel something else. I feel drawn to her by the most powerful feeling—and I know that I must have my wicked way with her. Her eyes lower to my lips.

"Raphael Monstrum, please come in." I go to let go of her hand, but she still has a tight grip on me. I have this girl's head in a spin. I look down and see parts of her hand have turned white from her grip. I don't feel any discomfort; this girl wouldn't be able to cause me any harm. I cannot stop an amused laugh from escaping my lips and yank my hand back. She looks confused and then it dawns on her. Now the games begin.

I walk off down the hall and into the dining room, leaving her to shut the front door. I personally put that door in, and I know that she won't be able to close it. I hear as she struggles, and as much as I would love to stand here and listen, I go and help her. When I step into the hallway, quite a scene greets me. Rosannah's back is to the door, and she is pushing with all her might. Her face is screwed up in the funniest expression, and I try my hardest not to laugh. She opens her eyes and sees me standing there. I startle her and it makes it all the more amusing.

"I am terribly sorry about that, how rude of me. Here," I say as I walk over to her. She doesn't look too impressed. It's not for your entertainment, darling. I can't resist another opportunity to touch her and use the back of my hand to move her out of the way. That strong, magnetising pull again. I get distracted and shut the door with my other hand forgetting my facade. She looks at my arm and then down at my chest. She then looks back at me and frowns. Is she on to me? Damn. "Follow me." I smile trying to hide my concern. I head back into the dining room once more, and she follows me like a little lap dog. From this point on, I try to stay as far from her as I can without it looking strange. I do not want her to get any suspicions about me. Suspicions can lead to fear and fear can cause uncontrollable scenes, and I want Rosannah controlled.

I showed her around the house but only gave her a brief glimpse my bedroom. I know the time will come when I will truly let her venture in. I will have to see her again, push her a little further each time we meet. I need to wind her up ever so slowly, so I can sit back and watch the show. I don't have to try very hard to get her flustered, and flustered she is. She doesn't finish her questionnaire and doesn't even realise that I haven't shown her the garage or the garden in her hurry to escape. Once she's gone, I get straight on the phone. "Marie, I need to see Rosannah again tomorrow morning. She did not view the garden and garage. Send her to me," I all but demand.

"Certainly," she chirps. I hang up, knowing the task will be done.

CHAPTER FOUR

Rosannah

The following morning I'm on my way to Raphael's house again. I have already dropped Brianna off at work after another barrage of questions. She's made me practically promise to take a photo of him this time. I couldn't manage to get a sniff of him so how the heck am I going to sneak a picture? Apparently, my descriptions aren't enough for her, and if he's so gorgeous, she wants proof. I think she'll be waiting forever for that one. As I pull up to the gate, I look further down the road at the other break in the trees. It looks like the beginning of another drive. So, Raphael has a neighbour or neighbours. I pencil it into my mind to stop off later and ask some questions, even though I shouldn't. I can't help but be curious about the mystery that is Raphael. The gates open and I drive up the impressive drive to the house. The garage is actually open this time, and I'm amazed to see it's empty.

I park inside on the left. It's easily large enough to fit at least four cars in. I get out and lock Anthea, thinking that maybe Raphael isn't in. A pang of disappointment hits me. I have been secretly looking forward to this much more than I should.

"Well, hello again," I hear by my right ear. I spin around with fright and fall back to the car. Raphael, who has appeared out of nowhere, is in my face. Bent slightly forward with his arms behind his back. Had I not fallen backwards, our lips probably would have met! He was that close.

"Oh, God, you scared the hell out of me," I say breathlessly while I clutch at my throat, sprawled out against Anthea. His eyes quickly flick down at my hand and back up. A slightly darker edge takes over his features.

"Sorry to startle you. It's nice to see you again," he says, his face smoothing back to a smile. Stepping back, he holds out his hand. I look at it and remember how cold it was yesterday. I meekly take it with a slightly shaky palm. It's still cold, and there's still that undercurrent that charges through me. I look at his face; he is more beautiful than I remember. Not even my own memory can do his good looks any justice. It was only yesterday that I last saw him, but it feels like it's been too long. He's dressed in the same leather jacket as yesterday but is wearing black jeans and a dark green shirt. His grip tightens and my heart skips a beat. He pulls me back on my feet without any effort and shakes my hand. I look at his hand, amazed at how one of those could shut that monster of a front door.

"This is obviously the garage. I apologise for my forgetfulness in not showing it to you yesterday. I would also like to show you the garden, but first, let's go inside and sit." He smiles, grabbing my attention. He lets go of my hand and walks off through a door that's situated on the right side of the garage. I could have sworn it was shut when I drove in, but at least, my hand didn't go all bunny boiler on him this time. I nearly run after him to see where he's gone. The doorway comes through to the house, set back between the huge staircase and the dining room. I enter the hall just in time to see Raphael's billowing jacket disappearing around the corner towards the dining room. I realise that he's left me to close the door again. Where are his manners? Round the corner, picking up...this isn't the time for jokes.

The door looks heavy, so I press my two hands against it. I push with all my strength, but to my horror, it's quite light. It slams shut, taking me with it. Bang! Damn it! I curse myself. I'm now leaning against the door at quite a peculiar angle. Butt sticking out and legs askew. My handbag, which has fallen from my wrist slightly down my forearm, is swinging avidly in front of my face. Doing an awkward press up against the door, I manage to stand. I turn around with a bright red face only to see Raphael leaning against the wall with his arms crossed. He's trying to suppress a smile, but I can see that he wants to laugh. I can't ignore the little niggle in my head that's telling me that he wants to play games with me. Much to his amusement, he left me to shut the front door yesterday and left me to shut this one today. I narrow my eyes at him in suspicion, but he just carries on trying to suppress that smile, heading to the dining room.

Damn you, Raphael. Looking at the shut garage door, I can see why I didn't notice it yesterday. It blends in perfectly with the wall. Only the handle gives it away. I follow Raphael into the dining room, and we sit down. Again, Raphael creates what feels like the great divide between us.

"Would you like...anything?" he asks with deliberate anticipation. Is that inappropriate? I have no idea what he means, but it sure as hell has my heart racing. I have to use all my will to stop my eyebrows from shooting up.

"Oh, no thank you. I, err, need to see the garage," I say looking at him expectantly, even though that's where we've just come from. He sits there, looking at my features. I feel like there's a spotlight on me, my face feels the heat of his gaze. Or maybe I am just blushing, again. After what feels like an eternity, Raphael finally speaks.

"You've already seen it. It's forty foot wide and forty foot deep," he says, resting his eyes on mine. I stare at him for a moment. He's definitely playing games with me. The garage was one of the things that I have come specifically to assess. I'll go for the grounds. I haven't seen all of it, so he can't fob me off on that one. "The land is two acres with an extensive underground crypt that dates back to when this house was built. It is no big loss if you do not see the garden, but I insist on showing you the crypt. It is full of my ancestors," he says, waiting for my reaction.

There's a bloody crypt here? I go rigid as I try to hide my surprise. I don't think I'm doing such a good job, as he's staring at me amused. I think he's enjoying making me squirm. Right then, the sun shines brightly into the room, and it highlights his pale magnificence in an astounding way. I gasp loudly in awe. He's so pale but the translucency gives his skin the illusion of such depth. An infinity of creamy white. I want to ask him so many questions in this instance. 'Are you going to hide me away and drain me of all my blood?' is the main one that keeps ramming its way into my conscious mind over and over. Damn you, Brianna. I opt with just staring at him instead. He looks slightly horrified as if he knows what is running through my mind. I blush at my ridiculous assumptions. "Sorry about that, just one of those funny hiccups," I say with a quick grin, hoping that it will cover up my embarrassment and aid my blatant lie. "Shall we go and see the garden?" I press.

He looks slightly relieved and half smiles. But instead of getting up, he leans his right elbow on the back of the chair and slides his right knee onto the seat next to me. Opening his knees to me, he is now facing me directly. Don't look there, don't look there. He bites his bottom lip to stop himself smirking and looks down at his own lap. My eyes follow his. Damn it. He did that deliberately! I close my eyes trying to sort out my now erratic breathing. Once it's under control, I take a deep breath and open my eyes, focusing back on his face.

"Yes, certainly. But there are some things that I want to discuss first," he says with authority.

"Affirmative." I nod. Affirmative? He looks as surprised as I feel. Where the hell did that come from?

"I mean, yes. That's fine with me," I say putting on a smile.

"Are you sure that you do not want to do an army drill first? I can arrange one for you," he says with a darkly amused expression. I stare at him horrified. I can honestly die of embarrassment right here, right now. Pulling myself back together, I persevere on. Desperate to escape again.

"What did you want to discuss?" I say ignoring his playful expression.

"Well, I wanted to tell you more about the house. Why I live here on my own, where my parents are. I'm sure that you have questions," he says raising an eyebrow and inspecting the back of his right hand. God, yes, do I have questions! But those are not the kind of things that I should be discussing with him. I know that Raphael's personal life is a dangerous territory that I shouldn't trespass on, but it's like telling someone not to push the big red button. They know they shouldn't, but you know they will. Curiosity is a powerful thing. I restrain myself from letting the many questions that are starting to fill my mind spew out of my mouth and ponder for a minute or two on what to ask first.

I play it safe and opt for a sensible one. "Why do you live alone?" I ask with intrigue and wonder lacing my words.

"Well, my parents were killed quite tragically, and I have yet to find anyone who is, shall I say, right for me," he says with an intense stare.

"I'm sorry about your family," I say, feeling a little bereft for him. How devastating it must have been to lose both parents.

"Oh, it was some time ago." He lightly smiles.

"So, who had this house built?" I ask trying to lighten the mood.

"An old family member. A Von Smit. He made his money by buying and selling land. When he made enough, he had this house commissioned. It has not changed much since then with the exception of the garage, which used to be a stable, and some modern amenities. He also had two other houses built. My sister lives in one and my brothers in the other." He shrugs. I wonder if his siblings are as beautiful as he is, but I doubt it.

"How did the name Monstrum come into your family?" I ask with a little smile. I love listening to him talk when he's not taunting me. Something about his voice soothes me.

"My mother became a Monstrum when she married my father. The name means monster in Latin." He laughs like it's some kind of an inside joke.

"Speaking of Latin, what does that sign say on the entry gates?" I ask as the quote springs to mind.

"Oh, that." He smirks. "It means 'to come in...'" He cuts off and frowns. Even frowning, he's still beautiful. Someone then knocks at the front door. Crash, crash. I yelp as the sound cascades through the house. It sounds like it comes from everywhere at once.

"Does it have to be that loud?" I ask with my face scrunched up remembering it from the yesterday. With the sound ricocheting around the inside of my skull, I can't stop the question from flying out of my mouth.

"Wait here, I'll be back soon." He shoots me an apologetic smile. Rising up from his seat, he walks out of the room with his jacket rippling around him. I decide to walk around the room, glad I can concentrate on the decor. There really is nothing personal in here. Come to think of it, there are no photographs on show in the house at all. Only the painted portraits in the hall. No photos of his parents and none of him or his siblings growing up. I bet that

Raphael was the most adorable little boy, so where are the photos?

After a few minutes of wandering around the room, I sit back down. I hear a strangely muffled cry. What the heck was that? I gingerly get up and make my way to the door. I can hear quiet clipped talking coming from the kitchen, so I walk a little further and stop a couple of feet from the kitchen doorway. The doorway acts as a frame, blocking a lot of the view of the room. I take in as much of the scene as it will allow.

There's a man backing away to the right from something that I can't see. Sweat beads his forehead, and he looks petrified. So much so, that he doesn't notice me standing here. He has two little wounds on his neck weeping a trail of blood, staining his collar with a bright red. A stark contrast to the crisp white of his shirt. Then what he fears comes into view. It's Raphael, but a different Raphael. What is he doing? He's like a predator, a big and powerful animal. Trapping the terrified man with his gaze, his attention solely hones on his target. His shoulders are slightly hunched, and his eyes are dark and hungry. His mouth is a harsh line, and his nostrils are slightly flared.

He stalks forward on slow nimble feet. A stance he looks completely natural and at home in. His body language says that he can go in for the kill at any moment, like a snake waiting to strike a venomous bite. But yet, his hands are held out in front of him, palms up, almost in surrender. Wrapping the pretence of weakness around him like a cloak.

"Now, look, Harry, we can do this the easy way," he half smiles, "or we can do this the hard way." His voice is smooth, deep, and confident but has an incredibly darker underlying edge. This isn't the same man I was talking with ten minutes ago, this is someone entirely different. What the hell is going on?

"Raph, I don't want any trouble," Harry pleads, pushing his hands out towards Raphael. But something tells me that won't ward him off.

"You don't get to call me Raph!" he booms and opens his mouth to reveal two extremely sharp and very pointy extended fangs. It makes me jump and gasp. He turns to face me, his fangs nowhere to be seen, and his eyes a light grey once more. "What is it with people and the word 'wait'?" he asks quickly staring into space.

"How could I not hear that?" I ask incredulously. He glares menacingly at Harry, who whimpers then turns the look on me. I stand frozen unable to move. My feet rooted, feeling as one with the wooden floor. All my energy has rushed to my brain, which is in overdrive, trying to make sense of what I have just witnessed. Did I actually see fangs? I must have imagined them.

"Raphael, she's only a child," Harry cries in the background. Still looking at me, Raphael holds his finger out to Harry as if to tell him to be quiet, but instead, Harry passes out and crumples forward on the floor. Without so much as a glance, Raphael sidesteps him as he falls and then steps over him once he has landed. He slowly makes his way towards me.

"I-is he okay?" I manage to mumble finding my voice, looking at Harry, who is face down on the floor.

"Relax, he will be fine," he says dismissing my concern with a wave of his left hand. "He is just... asleep," he says with narrowed eyes.

"What is wrong with your teeth?" I ask feeling slightly braver. "They looked like..."

"Fangs?" He finishes my question with a smirk.

"Yeah," I say, suddenly feeling stupid.

"That is because they are," he says with a sneer.

"You're insane!" I scream as I grab the kitchen door. Slamming it shut, I stumble backwards from the exertion. I'm thankful that my feet have decided to join the rest of my body. Suddenly, the door flings back open and it hits the wall with such force that it breaks into tiny pieces. I yelp out of shock and hold my arms up to shield myself from the scattering debris. I peek under my arms to see a light cloud of dust in the air. Once it's settled, I drop my arms and see Raphael standing in the doorway.

"Now, that was rude," he says looking unimpressed. I think about running, but the bravery I had before deserts me, and I can feel the colour drain from my face. My heart sinks as I make a brutal realisation. This man is a delusional maniac, and I'm within his grasp. Raphael closes the gap between us quite quickly. "So," he says towering over me. I can't look him in the eye, so I look down his body and at the floor. He lifts my chin with a cold finger, forcing me to look at him. He's slowly shaking his head. I feel a frantic fear rising up in me.

"Please don't kill me," I whimper.

"Well, I cannot have you telling every Tom, Dick, and..." he lets out a little laugh, "Harry."

"Even if I were crazy enough to tell anyone what you've just told me, they wouldn't believe me," I say slightly irritated.

"Believe me, Rosannah, there are people out there who would, and I cannot have that," he says with a sigh, letting go of my chin.

"But Harry will remember when he wakes up," I say feeling triumphant.

"Not only did I make him fall asleep, but I also erased some of his memory," he says. I deflate, and then take in what he actually said. He's a hypnotist? As well as a delusional maniac, don't forget about that.

"You can do that?" I ask suspiciously.

"Yes," he says deadpan.

"Oh, well why don't you do that to me then?" I ask. Smart arse!

"Trust me, I already tried. It didn't work," he says slightly irritated. Of course, it didn't work; do you think I'm stupid? But how does that explain Harry? Maybe he's an actor, but that's pretty elaborate to fake. Raphael looks grave and then grabs my arms.

"Oh God, what are you going to do to me?" I scream, filled with fear.

"I'm sorry; you know too much," he says calmly.

"No," I shout. Flailing around like a fish out of water, I try to wriggle free, but my effort is futile. His hands are like vices on my wrists. He's so much stronger than I am. Eventually, I give up struggling. He lets go, and I fall on my butt. Ouch!

"Grr," I growl and glare at him. He comes over and it looks like he's going to help me up but instead he picks me up bridal style and wraps me into his chest. He smells so good, like apples and spice. I breathe in deep and fill my lungs with his scent. Well, I now have confirmation that the Dracula room is indeed his bedroom. This will be my last thought before I die, great. I shut my eyes tight, and then he places me on something soft. I keep my eyes shut, afraid of what I might see if I open them. Clunk. I hear a lock turn into place. What was that? Never mind what I might see now! I open my eyes and realise I'm alone in a bedroom. The blue one. I run to the door and try to open it. It's locked, of course. I just heard it lock, but yet I still tried like an idiot. I start beating on the door with my fists, angrily screaming. Nothing. Feeling hopeless, I sink to the floor crying. What is he going to do with me?

CHAPTER FIVE

Raphael

I had counted the hours until Rosannah graced me with her presence once again. She was happy and contrite until Harry ruined it. Curse him! He is the reason I am now stuck in this predicament. I did not want her to find out. Well, not yet, anyway. Now, she is petrified of me, and Harry takes all the glory. That wonderful dancing light in her eyes and glow to her cheeks was mine to ruin when I saw fit! I am furious! The events cruelly roll through my mind once more as if to torture me once again.

"My mother became a Monstrum when she married my father. The name means monster in Latin." I laugh. If only she knew how fitting the name really is. Her face creases up a little in confusion. Yes, that is something you should remain confused about...for now.

"Speaking of Latin, what does that sign say on the entry gates?" she asks with her head slightly tilted to the side.

"Oh, that." I smile remembering its significance, especially to her. "It means to come in..." I stop at the sound of footsteps. Someone is coming to the house, and now really is not a good time. How did they get in? That's right, I left the gates open! I wait for the door knock and watch in amusement as my Pastel Candy girl cringes at the sound. I excuse myself, hoping she will actually listen to what I ask and wait. I know it is Harry before I open the door. I can hear his wheezing. I open the door and promptly pull him into the house. Shutting the door behind us, I whisk him into the kitchen. Before he can get his breath back, I action him to be silent.

"I have a guest," I sneer at him. He looks surprised but quickly the expression is gone.

"I'm terribly sorry Raphael, but it is an emergency. The 'you know what' has sent me here as there are more rumours going around," he whispers. I cannot stand Harry. Something about him just does not sit right with me.

"I have told you before; you need to bother Reggie with that shit!" I snarl at him.

"He won't listen, so I was sent to you as they knew you would help," he whispers back.

"Did you not listen to what I told you the last time you interrupted me with useless nonsense?" I growl. Unable to control my temper, I lunge. He makes a terrible sound like a pig squealing, and I let go immediately, jumping back away from him. Great, there is no way that Rosannah did not hear that!

"You need to leave. Now," I sneer at him.

"We haven't sorted anything out," he says through staggered breaths. I stalk towards him. "Now, look, Harry, we can do this the easy way," I smile, "or we can do this the hard way." I'd love you to pick the hard way; I will silence you in seconds!

"Raph, I don't want any trouble," he begs.

"You don't get to call me Raph!" I scream at him. Only people who know me very well can call me that. I hear a gasp and horror dawns on me. My anger disappeared instantly as I turn to see a horrified Rosannah. Damn it! I must have been so caught up in this ridiculous conversation that I did not even realise she was there! She must have heard Harry and came wandering even though I told her to bloody wait! "What is it with people and the word 'wait'?" I say to myself.

"How could I not hear that?" she asks me as if I am stupid. I turn and give my most aggressive look at Harry, who whimpers like a scared little girl. I then turn the look at Rosannah for talking to me like a fool. I can hear her breathing race faster and faster and watch her skin pale almost as much as mine.

"Raphael, she's only a child!" yelps Harry. I can really do with him shutting up!

I had left Harry on the floor and tried to deal with Rosannah. In her fear, she had tried to keep me at bay with a door. As if a door would stop me! I had destroyed it right in front of her. Believe it or not, I go through them quite frequently and have plenty of spares. I had approached her and tried to brainwash her after that, but to my surprise, it did not work. I have never come across anyone I could not brainwash. I knew then that she could never leave, and my plan had ultimately failed.

She had then tried to convince me that she would not tell anyone. But there are too many people out there with eager ears who would listen to anything she had to say about me. I could not let her go. As it dawned on her that she was stuck here, she started to freak out. She had caught me red-handed, with my pants down. Whatever 'phrase' you want to use, she had found out. Her reaction was not quite what I had expected. Maybe my ego had expected her to be impressed on some level. Oh no, not this female.

Instead of her swooning at my feet, I got a crazed, hysterical wailing girl. Tears and sobs everywhere.

Yes, I wanted that, but I wanted her smitten first. She even tried to fight me when I had to restrain her. Never underestimate my pure brute strength. With barely any effort, I wrapped her up in my arms, feeling her warm little body against my chest. She felt incredibly hot even through my shirt. I then did the only thing I could. I put her in a bedroom, locked the door, and ran away. Yes, I actually ran away. I would deal with her later, but I had to deal with Harry first. That all happened a few hours ago. I figure that Rosannah should have calmed down by now.

With Harry out of the way, I decide to tell her my story. I should tell her all the gory details, right? As I approach the door, I can hear that she has fallen asleep against the door. I rest my ear against the wood and listen to her. A slow, steady heartbeat drums in her little body, radiating through the door. I can smell the blood running through her veins, the perspiration from her exertion, and the tears from her sobbing. A sweet, salty, tangy, metallic smell blended with coconut, flowers, and alcohol. I unlock the door and hear her jerk awake. Grinning to myself, I hear her jump up and scurry to the other side of the room.

I have entered and locked the door again before she turns back around. I try my best to stifle a laugh. She is quite the sight. She has sleep caught in her eyelashes like little flies caught in cobwebs. Her eyes are brimming with red from crying. Half of her face and right forearm are red from where they have been joined together in slumber. She looks at me stunned. Yes, love, so you should be! She still looks a little alarmed so I decide on a calm, smooth approach. "I am only here to talk," I say holding my hands up to her. She sizes me up with her eyes, and I can see her mind working overtime, deciding whether she should trust me or not. She shouldn't.

She gives up and slumps down onto the bed, staring at me. Right, I guess that is the signal to go ahead. "I guess you have a lot more questions now?" I ask slightly frowning. I can see the pure judgement in her eyes. She despises me. I can see and feel the hate, but for reasons unbeknown to me, I cannot enjoy it as much as I would like to. She says nothing so I continue. "All of what I have told you so far is actually true. I have just left some details out. Telling you the full truth would have been a bad idea for obvious reasons. Do you have any questions you would like to ask?" I ask her, hoping that she will speak. I am beginning to think that she is in shock, but then she clears her throat.

"When can I leave here?" she asks deadpan. I smile inwardly.

"I will have to explain that to you later as it is a little bit complicated." I shrug.

"Okay, how old are you?" she asks, still in monotone. Good, something easy to answer.

"I am three hundred years old. I died when I was twenty-six," I say watching her carefully. Her eyes flicker across my face, but that is all the response I get.

"So, you haven't always been a....vampire?" she asks unimpressed.

"No, I was born March 23rd, 1713. I became a vampire in 1739," I say looking at her. She peers at the floor and starts to fiddle with her fingers. Is she bored? There is no way she can be bored, right?

"How did you become one?" she asks without looking up at me. I go over to the bed and sit down. She shuffles away from me. I am sitting right next to her; a couple of inches really does not make any difference. I look down at her fingers and frown. The story I am about to tell her is a really unpalatable one and for some inexplicable reason, it bothers me.

"Prepare yourself. This is not a fairy tale with a prince and a happily ever after," I say looking at the bedroom door. I see her look up at me in my peripheral vision. That got her attention, didn't it? "My transformation was not a very pleasant one. My life up until that point had been joyous, peaceful, and serene. It was full of vitality and zest. I had two loving parents, wonderful twin brothers, and a doting sister. I was the eldest, and unlike most siblings, we all got on incredibly well." I smile. "But good things are not meant to last."

My eyes narrow and are no longer focusing on what is in front of me. I slip into a daydream. "It was a lovely sunny Sunday afternoon. My parents had travelled here to discuss things with my grandparents. My siblings and I stayed at home, which was rare but just seemed to happen that day. My brothers, sister, and I waved our parents off as they rode out into the horizon. The sky was a sparkling background of blue, purple, and orange. It was the perfect image, a perfect moment, that would have made the most beautiful and wonderful photograph, had they existed. I would have welcomed that as the last sighting of my parents.

For them to disappear and for me to never know what happened to them.

"We waited for them to return, and by the following day, there was no sign of them. I knew something was terribly wrong. I wanted to come here to see what could have kept them, but my brothers and sister insisted on coming with me. And so, we journeyed here, and when we arrived, we were greeted with an eerie silence. The place looked the same, but the partially open front door betrayed the impression that everything was fine. I wanted to come in and investigate. Again, my brothers and sister insisted they joined me. I agreed, as long as they followed me. I gingerly opened the door, ventured inside, and witnessed with the most horrendous scene. My parents' and grandparent's bodies ripped to pieces, parts of them lay scattered around the downstairs hallway. There was no blood. I searched across a sea of body parts, and I caught sight of my mother's head. It was by the skirting board between the entertaining room and where is now the TV room. It was facing up to the ceiling as if she was looking into heaven, but it was just an illusion.

"Her eyes were glazed over, and her face frozen in contorted agony. I could not stop the bile that rose up my throat and spewed out of my mouth. It splattered spectacularly onto the floor, across my shoes, and onto the bottom of my pants. I heard gasps and gags behind me, and I knew that the others had seen as well. The candle in the hallway, which was still burning, flickered and cast demonic shadows across the walls. I sank to my knees and began to sob. Who would do such thing? Who could do such a thing? I was broken from my sobs by a deep, evil, demonic laugh. I jumped up and turned around to see two figures in the shadows on the stairs. The monsters had murdered my family. I charged to where they were but a hand around my throat suddenly stopped me. I was lifted off the floor. My captor had a veil across their face so I could not look into their eyes. I kicked my legs about as I struggled for air. Just as I was sure I would pass out, I was placed back on the floor and my arms were tightly gripped. I sucked in deep breaths now that my throat was free. I looked over and stared into the terrified faces of my sister and brothers. 'Run,' I managed to get out between breaths, and they bolted. A vicious voice from behind the veil spoke. 'Your family had to go, and you were too but seeing how much you enjoyed finding your family like this, another idea has entered into my mind.' Another voice behind me cackled. 'Go after them, you know what to do,' my captor told the other. I felt a wind whip around me but did not see anyone leave.

"'Now, to sort you out. You are going to remember this for as long as you live,' he said, and with that, my captor let go of one arm and leant forward. Biting me on my neck, I felt a sharp piercing pain. Once their teeth were in my flesh, they locked shut and ripped back out tearing through sinew. Blood splattered onto my face and across the floor in front of me. I went numb and limp due to shock. My captor held me up as I sagged in their arms. Then I felt something pressed against my neck and I thought that maybe they were trying to save me, but after a while, they let go of me and I collapsed onto the floor. I could see my own blood pooling on the floor in front of my face. I struggled to breathe, taking sharp, haggard, shallow breaths. I knew I was dying, my heart was trying its best to pump, but it was pumping my blood out of the wound in my neck. Suddenly, my sister was lying next to me. Blood dotted across her colourless face and the most horrific wound to her neck.

"'Now you can watch each other die. Enjoy it while it lasts,' sneered one of the monsters and then the only sound was us gasping for air. I could hear my brothers though I could not see them. Instead, I watched as the light faded out of my sister's eyes, and they glazed over. I tried to cry, but I did not have the energy to do so. I laid there for goodness knows how long gasping. Eventually, everything went black, everything stopped working, and I existed no more. I was nothing. I was nowhere. Then I came back. I was in my mind again, in just blackness at first. I tried to open my eyes, but it was such a task. When I finally managed to open them, I felt the most extraordinary pain. Every bone in my body felt like it was breaking over and over and every cell of my being felt like it was on fire. I could not move and had to writhe there for hours in excruciating pain while my family lay dead around me. It was pure torture.

"I honestly thought I had died and gone to hell. I began to wonder what I had done in life to deserve such a fate. I stared at my lifeless sister who just stared back. I could not tell if anyone was behind those eyes or not. They looked a light grey, and I assumed she was dead, part of my own personal hell. Eventually, the pain eased, and I was able to move. I got up, and my eyes adjusted to my surroundings. It was unbelievable. The definition of everything was astounding. I could see everything—really see everything. I could see the grain of the wooden floor and the weave of my cotton shirt. It was all so much clearer. I heard a shift and turned to see my brothers standing behind me. They, too, had grey eyes.

"'Get back, demons of hell!' I yelled at them. 'Demons of hell? You are a demon of hell!' they yelled back in unison. I ran to the bathroom upstairs and reached it a lot quicker than I used to, but I was too dazed by the man who stared back at me from the mirror to pay any more attention to that. The image was as white as a ghost, and my once dark brown eyes were light grey. Suddenly, my brothers appeared beside me. 'See, a demon you have become!' they exclaimed. Seeing themselves in the mirror, a realisation hit them. 'Oh, my dear Lord. We, too, are demons of hell!' they wailed. We turned to look at each other. 'I do not understand what has happened to us. It looks like we have landed in hell, but yet, everything seems so much better. Sight and...' I broke off to race downstairs. Wind whipped around me and my brothers were with me again. 'Speed.' We all just looked at each other and then waited, hoping our sister would wake up, too.

"When she did, we explained what we had found out so far. She was the calmest about everything. We then decided to notify the authorities, only telling them that we had found our family murdered, of course. How would they believe the rest? It turned out that my uncle's family had been murdered, too. There were only the four of us left. I, being the eldest, inherited everything, which I then shared with my siblings. There was an incredible amount of money and three properties—this one, my parents' house, and my uncle's house. I took this place and let the other three fight it out over who got the other two. My sister claimed our parents' house while my brothers took our uncle's." I look at Rosannah, who now appears to be quite shocked.

I look away and continue. "We were not checked out by a doctor because our wounds had healed. There appeared to be nothing wrong with us, apart from our eyes. The people of the town thought our eyes had been damaged by what we had seen, but we could see better than we could ever have imagined. We had no idea that we were actually vampires, and we tried to live our normal lives while still dealing with a pure and solid grief. We tried to put the madness of it all behind us and pretend it was not real, but that did not last very long. We soon discovered that although we could draw in air, we could also stop breathing—for hours, days, weeks even—and still live. We could not, however, eat or drink anything. We threw it all up every time we tried. We did not feel ill, and yet, there was no explanation. We remained incredibly pale even though we went outside in the sun. We were wasting away yet not dying. We were literally walking skeletons. Rumours began to circulate about us being possessed by demons and being the undead. We became recluses to hide away from judgemental eyes. We hoped that we would just die, hidden away from everyone." I pause. "It was not living; it was a cruel excuse for existence!" I shout.

Rosannah whimpers a little, and I shoot her an apologetic smile. Why the hell do I even care? She is meant to be scared. I sit in silence for a while contemplating this. "So, how did you find out you were vampires?" she asks with a slightly sarcastic tone. "Well, two men turned up at my doorstep one day, and after ignoring their incessant knocking, I eventually answered. I noticed that they bore my own paleness and light grey eyes, and then I realised just how I must have appeared to other people. It is one thing looking into a mirror and seeing it as just an image you can walk away from, but it is another to see it in the flesh right in front of you.

"They introduced themselves as Mathias and Porticus and asked to come in. I found their names strange, and I did not like the look of them, but I had nothing to lose. If they killed me, it was a bonus. I led them into the dining room. They started by saying that they knew what had happened to me and that they had something I would be able to drink. They produced a pretty glass bottle with a thick red liquid in it. They told me it was blood, and that I was a vampire. I was dismayed and marched to the front door. Holding it open, I told them to get out. They sauntered off, telling me they would be back very soon. When I went back into the dining room, I saw that they had left the blood.

I ran back to the front door, but when I opened it, they were nowhere to be seen. I went back to the bottle and eventually poured myself a glass. I could not believe it had come to this. It took me five hours of warring with myself before I took the first sip. A simple red fluid that mocked and ridiculed me.

Although normal food still tasted the same, this tasted so much better. Conflict and disgust thrown aside, I downed the rest of the glass. I expected to throw it up, but to my surprise, I stomached it. I then went to my brothers and sister with the bottle and got them to try it without telling them what it was. They were so delighted with it that they were not bothered once I told them what it was." I smile.

"Did those two men come back?" Rosannah asks.

"Yes, and they explained all about vampires and their abilities to us. Like brainwashing. We had to learn to get over the guilt of feeding off of people and have the ability to make them forget," I say with glee.

"Did they ever catch those who did this to you?" Rosannah asks clearly confused.

"Unfortunately not, but I hounded Mathias and Porticus to set up something in place to kind of 'police' vampires. And thus, the vampire synod was born." I shrug.

"Did you not ever find love?" she asks. I can see the pity all over her face.

"The closest was Emily. We were engaged at the time of my death. Once I knew I was a vampire, I tried to carry on courting her, but it was near impossible. She always noticed that I did not eat or drink, always commented on my pale complexion and grey eyes. I tried to be normal, human, but one day, I forgot and whipped around in front of her. It almost scared her to death. She ran off and I did not have it in me to chase after her. I felt certain people would know and feared they would come with their pitchforks and torches. But Emily left this town and never spoke a word of what she had seen to anyone,"

I say. Wondering what the hell I am going to do with Rosannah, I do not look at her as I get up and walk out of the room. Locking the door behind me, I head downstairs to my study. I need to make some phone calls.

CHAPTER SIX

Rosannah

After Raphael leaves, I just lay on the bed for what feels like ages, staring up at the ceiling. I knew Raphael was too good to be true. I thought I had finally found the man of my dreams, but life has a funny way of being ironic. Why does the most handsome man I have ever seen turn out to be a complete and utter nutjob? I have never been attracted to anyone unless you counted poor Mickey McDonohue. In nursery, I used to bash him over the head with my Barbie. I could never explain why I always had this urge to hit him whenever I saw his face. When I grew older, I assumed it was just a silly crush, but according to my mother, he was my first love.

"It was love at first sight. It brought tears to my eyes. His parents were stinking rich. I knew my little girl had developed an eye for the rich ones, and at such an early age! But then, you ruined it when you didn't pursue him any longer. When I asked the teachers about it, they claimed it was a phase that you had outgrown, but I knew different," she had said to me once on the phone when I had joked about Mickey.

You see, she had pointed out that I had never had a boyfriend, as she had done many times in the past, and I thought it would be a laugh to mention him. Big mistake. That was what brought on the whole 'gay' incident. She started thinking, which could be a very

61

dangerous thing. Later the same day that we'd had our chat about Mickey, she had turned up at my flat unannounced. I knew it was her before I opened the door. She holds the bell for ages, causing a terrible long shrilling ring. My poor neighbours. I knew that I was about to get the third degree over something.

My mother never visits unless it's what she considers an emergency, and when it comes to those, we are never on the same page. If I had known what I was in for, I would have pretended that I was out, but that would have only delayed the inevitable. My mother would wait for all eternity if she had to. "Rosannah," she had greeted me in her usual monotone. "Come in, Mother," I said while I held open the door for her as she flounced in. I watched as she walked past Marmalade. "Cat." She nodded at her. I glared at the back of her head as she made her way to my seat. She knew it was mine because I had pointed it out when she had once asked. She has sat on it every time she has come over since. God, please help me and forgive me my sins... I thought as I looked skyward. I'm not a religious person, but I honestly think my mother could get anyone praying to God.

My mother had sat in my seat sighing and huffing away. You'd have thought it was the end of the world... Poor Marmalade just ran and hid. If only I could have done the same.

"Rosannah, I have been thinking since our phone call today, and I have been quite disturbed by the conclusion I have come to." Great, another two plus two equals five. And it only took her twenty minutes this time. "I know why you haven't had any boyfriends in your life," she stated.

"Really? Do enlighten me, as there's no way I'd possibly know why," I said as sweetly as I could. She never accepted the fact that I couldn't find anyone I liked; according to her, I had turned them all away. With her, there always has to be a reason why other than the truth. She actually said those things in the past. Number one, I was too picky and let an incredibly ugly face and equally ugly personality get in the way. Number two, I let the fact that I was four get in the way. Number three, I valued my virginity too much. Number four, I liked to sabotage her attempts at finding me a man. Number five, I let my self-respect get in the way when she'd have no problem bewitching a man for her own greed. A man, I might add, who she had married purely to divorce and take his fortune and life's work. Poor guy was ruined. He lost everything and everyone and killed himself in the end. Number six, I must have too many of my father's genes because I haven't followed in her footsteps. And my personal favourite, not. Number seven. Jumping back to mother's unexpected visit.

"You're gay," she stated. I nearly choked on my own saliva. "You're seeing women behind my back while trying to pretend that you're straight. Your life is over. I'll never have a son-in-law or any grandchildren," she said as started to sob. She actually cried! She pulled out a handkerchief from her Luis Vuitton handbag and started to blow her nose quite dramatically. I was dumbfounded. It wasn't because it was untrue that I found it so shocking, but the fact that she was so against it.

"Mum, do you hear yourself?" I asked her incredulously.

"Yes, I do, perfectly clear. It hit me like a ton of bricks after you put the phone down earlier. It was absolutely awful. You have had no boyfriends and any chance you've had with any guy has been sabotaged. It must be because you're gay," she blubbered as she continued to sob. The audacity of it!

"That is the most ridiculous thing I have ever heard!" I said astoundedly. I never thought she'd be able to trump the last reason, but right there, she had managed to trump them all. "I have never given you any inclination that I was gay, apart from the fact that I've never had a boyfriend, which I might add, I have explained to you. All the men I've come across have been complete jerks. As soon as they realise I'm not putting out, they can't get away fast enough. Besides, there is absolutely nothing wrong with being gay! If I were, which I most definitely am not, I wouldn't be ashamed of it, and I certainly wouldn't hide it from anyone. So what if you had a daughter-in-law instead of a son-in-law? And as for grandchildren, there are other ways. Two people in love is a very beautiful thing and sex should not dictate who can and can't love each other! Honestly, seeing women behind your back? What the hell will you think of next?" I had ranted, throwing my arms up in the air causing Marmalade, who had just decided to pop out of her little hiding place, to jump and scurry back.

"So, you're not?" my mother had asked beaming at me, black mascara smudged around her eyes making her look like a female OAP member of Kiss. She was so happy that she hadn't even noticed I'd used the word hell in front of her. That usually warranted a telling off.

"No, Mother, and don't ever let Uncle Max hear any of your anti-gay nonsense," I warned her.

"Oh, I was only anti it if you were one." She smiled at me. She still didn't get it, and I wasn't going to bother and try to explain it again. She was ecstatic that I wasn't gay, but I was ashamed of her about it and made her swear never to mention the conversation again. She promised, but I know she still thinks I'm gay, even though she won't say it anymore. The thought will still bump around in her head for as long as I don't have a boyfriend. To her, it's the perfect explanation. She always made out that there was a problem with me when they'd only been problems to her. It was all meant to be part of her plan to get her a rich and handsome son-in-law and beautiful grand kiddies. But her talks were so wrong on so many levels.

Yes, she meant for the 'gay' incident to be one of her pep talks, but she did what she always did. She tried to excuse her terrible behaviour with the guise of looking out for me. In one of her other pep talks, she had once told me that she was already having sex when she was fifteen. It was as mortifying as it sounds. Listening to your mother telling you about all the sizable meat she'd had over the years was completely nauseating. And as if that wasn't bad enough, she had then told me that my father had been the best she'd ever have and that was what upset her the most about him was that she, and I quote, 'wouldn't get to bang him again because he ran off.' I was not surprised! And here I am, trapped in one of Raphael's bedrooms, thinking about all of this nonsense.

I honestly should be thinking of trying to escape or trying to get some kind of help. But I don't think my situation has entirely sunk in yet. Instead, I'm thinking about silly things that are making me feel quite wretched. I'm broken from my thoughts by the door unlocking. Clunk. Raphael is back.

I sit up on the edge of the bed. In a flash, the door opens and closes. Four figures are standing in front of the door, all eyes on me. I really am seeing things. People don't move that fast. Okay, so it isn't just Raphael. He's here, of course, but there are three others. All incredibly pale. There is a set of identical twins. They look a lot like Raphael, same facial structure but with some baby fat. They're not as built or as tall as he is but you wouldn't want to mess with them. They appear to be a couple of years younger than he is. Or frozen a couple of years younger than him, if I'm to believe any of Raphael's crap. They have the same light grey eyes and long dark hair except theirs is cut off at the shoulder. They are gorgeous, but not as stunning as Raphael. I don't think anyone could beat or even come close to his beauty.

The twins are dressed in different outfits. The one on the left is in black jeans and a white t-shirt that has a huge black logo on it stating 'never say never'. How very deep. The other one is in dark blue jeans and a black James Bond t-shirt. Next to them stands a woman. Her dark hair is up in a slick, high ponytail and it snakes its way down the right side of her neck, coming to rest mid stomach. She's in dark blue skinny jeans and a white broderie anglais vest with a mid-brown cardigan that buttons at the breast. She's incredibly beautiful and looks very similar to the others. The same facial features, but she's shorter and more petite. She looks about my size.

Walking with such precision, one of the gorgeous twins comes over to me, the one with the Bond t-shirt. It looks like I'm going to get a closer look at him. His light grey eyes are clear as glass. His face is a flawless piece of art—a smooth and bright canvas. His skin is almost transparent like Raphael's. His dark hair rich and full. He has a cheeky glint in his eyes that has me slightly wary of him. He comes to a stop inches away from my knees. As he lowers in front of me, I pull my head back instinctively. Once at eye level in front of me, he looks deep into my eyes. In my peripheral, I can see the others eagerly watching. It's strange, it's like he's looking beyond me, trying to see something that isn't there.

"You're right," he whispers so quietly I can barely hear him. I see a flicker of movement out of the corner of my eye and could swear Raphael just nodded. My imagination is playing tricks on me again. There's no way he could have heard that. Suddenly, the twin prods me with a super sharp nail on my cheek.

"Ow!" I yell pulling my hand up to my face so fast that I almost slap myself. In the blink of an eye, he's suddenly back to where the rest of them are. What? This place is doing things to my mind.

"Lawrence, what have I told you about poking the guests!" Raphael shouts. The other twin sniggers. Raphael throws him a daggered look and he stops. "Sorry about that. Lawrence has a funny way of saying hello," Raphael says apologetically while shooting Lawrence a glare.

"Well, I'm not a monster with two heads, you know," I scorn rubbing my cheek.

"She's a feisty one," says the sniggering twin with a smirk, but before Raphael could chastise him, the woman steps forward.

"I think she's beautiful." She grins at me before turning to Raphael. "Are we keeping her or are you going to do what you usually do?" she chirps. I'm horrified. Keep me? What does he do instead?

"Yes, we have to keep her," Raphael says with a bit of a regret in his voice. "Right," he says quickly clapping his hands together and making me jump. He walks out in front of everyone. "This is Rosannah." He points to me, and they all focus on me. "Let me introduce you to my family." He holds out his right hand. "These are my twin brothers, Lawrence and Nicholas. They are quite the nuisance. You have to watch your back with these two around, especially Lawrence," he says with a knowing grin. The twins both snigger. "And this is our baby sister, Evangeline." She scowls at him. "And we are all vampires," Raphael says to which they all smile. Wow, all four of them believe that they are vampires. Either they're a crazy family who is as nuts as each other or something incredibly bizarre is going on. I really don't know what to think anymore.

"Well, considering my brother is holding you captive, and you have no clothes, you can borrow some of mine. You look about my size," Evangeline says sizing me up with her eyes. How thoughtful. When I don't respond, she rushes over to me and literally pulls me off the bed. "Ow!" I yelp as my shoulder pops. "Oh, I'm so sorry. I have to be gentler with you. Guess I don't know my own strength." She giggles pulling me out of the room and into one of the bedrooms at the back of the house. Once there, I am faced with more pink than anyone should ever have to witness. The walls, the curtains, everything, is plastered in pink. The only things that are spared this fate are the wooden floor and the furniture. I don't remember this room looking like this the last time I saw it. I could have sworn it was a rich royal red before. I don't know what I'm thinking anymore. "You look utterly lost." She giggles at me. That's because I feel utterly lost.

"This room, I could have sworn it was different yesterday," I murmur looking at everything in sight.

"I asked Raph to decorate it for me as I will sometimes be staying. You know, to keep you sane. He said no, but I did it anyway." She shrugs. It's too late for my sanity now!

"But, how? That fast?" I murmur.

"Never mind that, see what you like in amongst this stuff." She opens the doors to a huge wardrobe. There are piles and piles of clothes in there. "Take what you want. I have plenty." She grins tipping her head to the side. I opt for the simplest of things.

"Erm, just vests and jeans will do," I say staring at the ridiculous amount of clothes in front of me. She starts to pull random vests and jeans out and piles them onto the bed. I know Raphael's story, but I want to see if Evangeline can match it. There has to be a discrepancy somewhere. "So, Raphael has always lived on his own?" I risk asking.

"Yes, well since our family was killed. That was two hundred and seventy-four years ago. Up until then we all lived in what used to be our parents' house. It's been my house since their death." She smiles while still pulling out more clothes and adding them to the pile. The math adds up.

"So, he never met anyone, a vampire lady?" I ask, cringing at the madness of my question. She sighs. Grabbing both of my hands, she sits down on the bed and pulls me down to sit next to her. Her hands are cold like Raphael's. Were her hands cold when she pulled me off of the bed before? I can't remember. I was too busy being in shock.

"You like him," she states, breaking me from my thoughts. Yeah, if I really love incredibly gorgeous deranged lunatics!

"Well, err, he's definitely something special," I say trying to grin and evade her penetrating stare.

"He's good looking and all the girls like him so I wouldn't blame you if you did," she smirks. All the girls? How many are there?

"So, you're telling me that I'm a statistic?" I ask her plainly.

"No, I'm telling you that you like him," she says and leans closer to me. "And you didn't even deny it," she whispers. I grimace. She has a point. Why didn't I at least try? "Don't worry, I won't tell him," she says winking slowly at me. "Right, I'll get the rest of the vests and jeans for you." She grins as she gets up. I turn to look out of the window. I can see that it's a beautiful sunny day. I remember Raphael telling me that he was able to go out in the sun when he discovered he was a vampire. He had to come up with something. Earlier in the dining room, the sun shone through the window and he didn't burst into flames. How can he possibly expect me to believe that vampires exist and can walk in the sun? I don't believe a single thing any of them has told me apart from their bloody names! They're only pale because they don't go out in the sun much. I turn back to Evangeline to see that she has pulled so much stuff out. "Stand," she commands and then piles me up with them. They're heavy and my arms sag under the weight. "I've thrown some jumpers and cardigans in there, too," I hear her say.

"Mft," I reply as the clothes are blocking my mouth.

"Oh, right. I'll guide you back to your room," she says with a giggle. She grabs my shoulders and guides me back to my dungeon. I try to put the clothes on the bed neatly, but they fall into a heap. I turn around to see that only Raphael has waited. "She's a jeans and vests kind of girl. No underwear, though." Evangeline giggles. The twins laugh in unison from somewhere in the house. Raphael raises his eyebrows at me. I go bright red and look at the floor. How could I have forgotten about that? "Don't worry. I've put a few new packs of panties and socks in your wardrobe, and we'll shop online to get some bras," she whispers to me. Raphael smirks and leaves the room. Great, now he thinks I'm a commando girl. I turn around and throw myself face down onto the bed. Hearing Evangeline's giggles fade away into the distance, I let out a huge sigh into the bedding. Why has this happened to me?

CHAPTER SEVEN

Raphael

Grinning to myself, I walk out of the bedroom and down to the kitchen. This is where we all end up when we need to discuss anything. Soon enough, Evangeline and the twins turn up. I did not necessarily tell them everything before. Just that there was someone I could not brainwash. Now they know the evaluation went terribly wrong.

"Raphael, are you insane?" Evangeline spits at me. She has changed her tune. She seemed pretty happy that she was here two minutes ago.

"What the hell are you on about? Brain got into its usual tangle?" I ask without looking at her.

"You told her? You actually told her? An employee at the estate agents, of all people!" she says incredulously. I turn to face her and grip my hands behind my back tightly as my anger boils up inside of me. She never asks what has happened; she always makes senseless assumptions.

"It is not like I shouted it from the rooftops. She saw me, but to be honest, I had a feeling she was suspicious before that," I say, my attention diverting to the twins who have sat at the breakfast bar eagerly watching us, hoping for a full-blown fight. The twins do not usually get involved. They normally watch and bet on who will win. They have kept quiet this time, but I know they are betting. Their hand signals are a giveaway. They both agree that Evangeline will win this time. My baby sister may look little and weak but

73

do not let that fool you. She is as strong as the rest of us but winning a fight is always down to outwitting the other. I am smarter, so I have the upper hand, but I do not want to fight right now. The Twins must think I have nothing to come back with if they believe Evangeline is going to win.

"Why the hell did you show her?" she asks.

"Harry was here," I say deadpan.

"You invited him over with Rosannah here?" she asks raising her eyebrows. Sometimes Evangeline is a bit of a challenge.

"How stupid do you think I am? He turned up uninvited. I whisked him into the kitchen where he provoked me. You know how much I cannot stand that little runt!" I shout. At this point, I am ready to lunge at her, but I calm myself and smooth my shirt down. "I told Rosannah to wait, but her curiosity got the better of her. I tried to make her forget, but it did not work. Like I said earlier, I cannot brainwash her." I sigh.

"I can vouch for that. I tried it out myself, and it doesn't work," pipes up Lawrence. Of all the things to butt in with, he butts in with that?

"I see. But was it such a wise idea to invite her here in the first place? I knew it was a bad idea when you said you wanted this house evaluated, but I knew it was an even worse idea when you told me you wanted her to come back a second time," she says crossing her arms. I look down at the floor and admit the truth.

"I had targeted her," I whisper, my eyebrows knotted together. I hate admitting my inner most desires.

"Oh. Oooooooh," she says as the penny drops. "A plaything." She smiles knowingly. I look away feeling slightly ashamed surprisingly. "Well, moving on, what we are going to do?" she asks. I snap my eyes to hers.

"You will do nothing. Rosannah is a hostage until either she dies or someone manages to make her forget what has happened. No one else is to know about this until I get to the bottom of why she cannot be brainwashed," I state at her.

"But..." she whines.

"No buts, Evangeline. You are all to go back home. Only fleeting visits...and I have seen what you have done to my royal red room," I say disgusted.

"But..." they all say.

"She is not your play buddy." I point at a pouting Evangeline. "And she is not for your betting amusement." I point at the twins who snigger. "She is mine," I growl. "I am going to my study; I expect you all gone by the time I re-emerge," I say over my shoulder as I leave the room. I whisk off to the study and shut the door before they can argue. Ten minutes later, I hear a group approach the house. It sounds like...it cannot be, surely? I listen incredulously as Evangeline lets them in and takes them to the dining room. For her sake, she better not have invited them over. In a few significant strides, I reach the door. Opening it, I race into the dining room to be faced with Evangeline, Twins, and The Synod, who are all standing around the table. All of them—Mathias, Vladimir, Bernadette, Reggie, and Porticus—are here. I gape at Evangeline, who is completely oblivious.

"This had better be good," Bernadette says begrudgingly.

"Raphael is harbouring an enormous risk," states Evangeline. They all look at me.

"Well, talk, dear boy, tell us what has happened," Mathias says encouragingly to me. I glare at Evangeline, but The Synod would have found out eventually. Taking people prisoner has always had consequences. I should know. I have been there before.

"That poor excuse for a human being turned up unexpected, spouting crap that concerns Reggie while Rosannah was here," I say reluctantly.

"Rosannah, hey?" Reggie taunts. I ignore him.

"He provoked me. Rosannah came looking for me, and she saw me." I look down. "In all my glory," I all but whisper. Laughter spreads through the room.

"Well, you know what you need to do. Make her forget. Honestly, calling us all here for something as simple as that," complains Porticus. I never wanted them all here! Now they can all get lost. They leave the twins, Evangeline, and I standing in silence. They are almost to the front door when Lawrence pipes up.

"Raphael can't do it," he says. What the hell? I hear their footsteps stop. Great. I shoot Lawrence a deathly glare, and he flinches slightly. The Synod all march back into the room, led by Vladimir.

"That's like a bull without its nuts!" He chuckles. They all join in.

"Jesus, it is only her that it does not work on. Lawrence cannot brainwash her either," I say feeling abashed.

"He's lying; they're all lying," snaps Reggie. Feeling somewhat insulted, I turn on him.

"Well, why not meet her and try it for yourself!" I say through gritted teeth. What the hell am I doing? I did not want them knowing about her and now I am inviting the worst of them to meet her!

"You two, stop this nonsense. If this is true, this is deadly serious. I've never come across anyone who couldn't be brainwashed. We must meet her to decide what to do with her. Clearly, she can't be let go. She knows way too much already," says Mathias.

"I say we just terminate her, cold and clean," shrugs Reggie.

"That will not be necessary, but I do not want her taken," I say, my eyes flicking quickly in Reggie's direction.

"Are you suggesting that we are not trustworthy, Raphael?" asks Porticus.

"No, but not everyone can be trusted," I reply.

"Raphael, you really need to stop judging Harry. Now go and get the girl," Mathias says. Did he completely ignore what Reggie said? I have no choice but to pull out my trump card.

"Might I advise you not to forget what is stored up here," I say through gritted teeth, tapping my temple. Mathias looks regretful and slowly nods.

"This cryptic crap again," Reggie sighs.

"We'll make it a vote. I know that this isn't our way of doing things, but I think we can make an exception," Mathias says, ignoring Reggie. Even though I can pull the upper hand, it is best not to flaunt it too much. One day the others will query what it is I know about Mathias that makes him run scared whenever I mention the secret he bestowed upon me all those years ago. I shall let this slide and allow the vote. Reggie will definitely vote against me. He is probably itching to have her away knowing how much it would anger me. The others couldn't care less, and to save time, will vote for her to stay here. If it is not profitable or worth their time, then they are not interested.

"Fine," I retort. They all nod at me except Reggie, who is not even glancing my way. I wave my hand at the table. "Take a seat but leave those three empty. I shall go and get her," I say as I point to three chairs at the head of the table. Turning away from them, I leave the room, and doubt enters my mind. Can I really put my faith in The Synod if they are happy to converge with the likes of Harry? I let him go, but I would have preferred to snuff him out, like a dancing flame on top of a candle. I would love to watch the light extinguish from behind his eyes. I did not want him having any knowledge of Rosannah. The punishment would be severe if I had killed him, so all I could do was brainwash him. But the more I do it, the more The Synod dislike it. Goodness knows what they were told to get them here. Evangeline and the twins have followed me out into the hall. "Make yourself useful and go get them something to drink, Evangeline," I demand. "And stay out of the way," I order at all of them.

"What about Rosannah?" Lawrence asks. I forget that she needs to eat.

"Knock something quick up for her, order something in if you have to. I do not care what it is just do it quickly," I growl.

"Raphael, it was a joint decision," Evangeline whispers. I know exactly what she is referring to, but why is she bothering to whisper? They can hear everything. Without saying another word, I head off upstairs to get Rosannah.

CHAPTER EIGHT

Rosannah

No sooner has Raphael left me does he return. Clunk. Hasn't he heard of knocking? It's only polite. The door opens, but Raphael stops in the doorway and doesn't enter. His face looks like thunder. What could have riled him up in such a short space of time?

"The Synod are here to meet you. Please make your way down to the dining room when you are ready. They are waiting to greet you," he says calmly and walks off leaving the door wide open. Who the hell are The Synod? A synod is some kind of government body, isn't it? How did they even get here so quickly? Maybe they live in the crypt. Maybe I should stop thinking! I freshen up in the en-suite and then make my way downstairs, not knowing what to expect. A room full of crazies springs to mind. I see that Evangeline and the twins are in the kitchen. They look a little sheepish. In too deep, are we?

With nerves bubbling to the surface, I enter the dining room. There's a group of people sat around the table. The lively engrossing conversation comes to a stop. I wonder what they were talking about. It sounded like crazy gibberish, but I can't shake the feeling that the topic of discussion was me. How do we fool her next? No doubt. I feel like a freak show. They stare at me, assessing me. Maybe they want to see if I'm crazy enough to join their ranks. Give it a bit more time in this nut house... I hope they have my size straight jacket, not!

"Please come and sit here," Raphael says as he motions to a seat next to him with his hand. I weigh up my options. Sitting next to a lunatic I've already met seems better than the ones I haven't. What pure madness. I make my way over to Raphael and sit. There's a bowl of soup and a plate of cake laid out at my place setting. So, vampires that can't eat food can cook? I look at all the other settings, and mine is the only one with food. They're going all out with this charade. Either that or they're going to poison me. Then I might wake up from this insane nightmare I'm trapped in. I could be at home in bed dreaming the whole thing up. The stupid thing is that if I'm dreaming, a small part of me wants Raphael to be part of the real world. Without the crazy, of course. Raphael leans over to me and my eyes flick to his luscious lips. "Introduce yourself to everyone," he whispers, his lips barely moving.

"Ventriloquist skills, too? My, my, Raphael, you have exceeded yourself," I whisper sarcastically to myself. Raphael frowns, and I hear muffled giggles from around the table. There is no way they heard that! I stand and stare at all the light grey eyes that gaze back. These fruitcakes must be regulars at contacts 'r' us. I bet they're on their reward scheme and everything. I narrow my eyes at them in suspicion. "I'm Rosannah," I say to them all and sit quickly back down. They murmur to each other except one guy. He looks at me with disgust. I instantly hate him.

"So, you can't be brainwashed?" he says with a sneer. Is this guy for real?

"You seriously want to brainwash me?" I ask sarcastically, narrowing my eyes at him. Brainwash me? Bitch, please. His lip curls and he glares at me. It's like a staring contest. Are you really trying to hypnotise me? He eventually gives up, and I smile with victory.

"I have come across thousands of humans over my years on this earth and there hasn't been a single one who couldn't be brainwashed. You are the only exception," he says spitefully. I glance at the others who all look concerned except Raphael. He's hiding a grin behind his right hand. The guy who just spoke to me then turns to Raphael. "Honestly, Raphael, where did you get this one from? I still think my earlier suggestion is the way to go," he says as if I'm not here. Earlier suggestion? I dread to even think. Raphael glares at him as he stands up.

"Please, eat first and then give me your votes afterwards," he says with disdain and sits back down. How can they eat? They have no food! And votes? What the hell can they be voting for? Which mental asylum to check into? I start to eat and ignore the little niggle inside my head that says it could be poisoned. I think I would welcome it right about now. All the others have something thick and dark red in their glasses. What could they use that looks like blood? "What?" Raphael whispers to me, noticing my stares.

"The red stuff?" I whisper back.

"Just eat," he says with a frown. I shove a spoonful of soup into my mouth almost sulking. The flavour hits me, and it's delicious. Minestrone, my favourite.

"We can hear you, you know," pipes up 'Mr. Look into my eyes'. He's taking this to a whole other level of crazy, which I didn't think was possible.

"It's nothing that concerns you, Reggie," Raphael says, flashing him a false smile. Reggie? I almost spit my mouthful of soup out and manage to contain the belly laugh threatening to make an appearance. A vampire called Reggie? You couldn't make this up if you tried! Well, they've managed it.

"My name is Regius, but everyone calls me Reggie," Reggie huffs, his upper lip twitching to reveal glinting red teeth. What could do that? Ribena? No way. Something very staining, like beetroot juice perhaps. But that wouldn't be thick enough.

"I'm terribly sorry, Regius," I apologise, deliberately using his full name.

"No harm done," he says with a glare. It's fine that I was shocked he wanted to brainwash me but find his name funny? Watch out! Great, looks like I've made myself an enemy. Something I neither need nor want in this place. I finish my soup in silence, not daring to say anything else that might upset Regius. Nobody else talks, either, and there's no interest in my food at all. It smelt and tasted so incredibly yummy. Maybe this cult is on a juice diet? Definitely a diet of something, that's for sure. The vampires continue drinking their blood. I try not to stare at them while they're drinking it, but I can't help it. They honestly believe it's real blood.

"Dear girl, what do you keep staring at?" says an older looking man opposite me. I can't quite put my finger on it, but something isn't right with him. I feign ignorance and go along with their stupid façade

"I just don't understand how you could drink that stuff," I answer with a flick of my hand.

"Well, it's like a very rare steak; we love the flavour. Besides, I think we are all done now," he says and bows his head to me. Of course, you love the taste, you bloody whacko! I bow my head in return. What the hell am I doing? "Right, time for your votes," he says. Are they really doing this? I don't know what they are voting for, but I'm sure it's illegal. A blond, tanned man stands and addresses us all. Ha! A tan! See, I won't fall for all your crap! He then holds his hands out in front of him to quieten down the simmer from the others. His palms and wrists reveal he has an awful fake tan. Oh, dear Lord!

"I'll go first. You all know who I am, but I'll still introduce myself. I am Vladimir, and I take care of the welfare of our species. I vote you stay here. I don't see any advantage to taking you away," he says with a smile. So, that's what the votes are for. Wait, the welfare of your species? He nods to Raphael and sits. A woman on his left stands up. She looks like she belongs in Edwardian times with her skirts and frills. Her brown hair is pinned up into a knot of curls.

"I am Bernadette. I am responsible for the equality of the females of our species. I vote you stay here. You are in no threat of sexism here," she says with an authoritarian tone. The others mumble as she sits back down. Sexism, seriously? The guy to her left stands up and puffs his chest out. He's the ancient looking one, with white thinning hair and spectacles. Why didn't I notice them before? See! If he were a real vampire, he wouldn't need glasses! I then realise there's no glass in them—they're just for show!

"I am Mathias, and I am the head of The Synod. I vote you stay here," he says and slumps back in his chair. It's like he's...defeated. That's strange. He's the head of these weirdos, so why would he behave like that? He's who Raphael was talking about when explaining the formation of The Synod. Why is he in charge and not Raphael? Will you listen to yourself! I wonder if Porticus is here, too. God, how can they all believe this? It jumps to the other side of the table. A handsome red-haired man stands up.

"I am Porticus, and I am in charge of the security of our species. I vote that as a matter of security, you come with us," he says and gives Raphael an apologetic smile. He sits back down. So, there he is. Of course, he'd be here. The others who have already voted mutter amongst themselves.

"Please be quiet, it's my turn," says a disgruntled Reggie. He doesn't bother to stand and stares at his nails. Tart. "I am Regius, AKA Reggie. I am responsible for illegal blood consumption. I vote you come with us." He glares at me then at Raphael. I look next to him and see that the chair between us is empty. Glad at that, I look at Raphael puzzled about this.

"I did not want anyone sitting next to you other than me," he whispers and stands. So, I can sit next your crazy ass but not theirs? Makes sense. "I am Raphael, the founder of The Synod, and I am responsible for the unlawful changing and killing of humans. I vote she stays," he says and sits.

"Well, it looks like the votes are on your side, Raph. She stays with you," says Mathias. Of course, they are! How could you all fake me being taken to your vampire headquarters!

"Rosannah, stay here. I shall see everyone out," Raphael says as Evangeline enters the room. She waits until everyone has left the room then she squeals and claps her hands together. Dashing over to me, she then grabs my hand and leads me out of the dining room.

"What about my cat? Someone needs to feed her." I frown. I have my priorities, right?

"Don't worry, Raph will sort that out," she chirps. As we make our way up the stairs, I watch Raphael talking to Porticus and Regius. He doesn't look very happy. They all turn to look at me, but Evangeline pulls me away. What could they be discussing? How to chop me up and make a stew out of me? If they're going to kill me, I really wish they would hurry up and get it over with. I don't think I can handle much more of this. Evangeline leads me back into my prison. "I've already ordered some bras for you. They'll be here in a couple of days. There's also some other bits in there, too." She grins.

"How did you know what size to order?" I ask, puzzled.

"The twins have the knack of being able to tell a woman's bra size just by looking at them. They're never wrong. For once, it's actually come in handy." She sighs. The twins laugh from somewhere inside the house. "I shall see you in the morning." She smiles and leaves the room, locking the door behind her. I lay on the bed for hours trying to stay awake but inevitably, sleep overtakes me.

CHAPTER NINE

Raphael

I meant for Rosannah to be my little secret, but I just couldn't keep it to myself, could I? Now they are involved. I remember the conversation I had with Reggie and Porticus before they left. I had just watched Evangeline pull Rosannah up the stairs. Turning back, a sneering Reggie faced me. "I know your game," I said, matching his sneer.

"If I had it my way, she'd be dead!" he spat at me and whisked off. Porticus grabbed my arm as I went to follow him.

"He's not worth it. He's just pissed that he was outvoted," he said, trying to calm me.

"Honestly, why did you vote no?" I asked turning my frustration on him.

"Raphael, if she escapes and blabs then we're all in the shit. Especially me. Besides, I knew the votes would go in your favour." He smiled apologetically.

"I know, Porticus. You're right." I sighed.

"See you at the next meeting." He grinned, and he was off, too, shutting the door behind him. When I go to bed, my last thought is about showing Rosannah the garden, especially the crypt. She is going to love it down there.

The following morning, a grinning Evangeline greets me in the kitchen. "I thought I told you that you weren't to be here all the time. I am showing Rosannah the garden and crypt this morning, and I expect you gone by the time she gets up," I tell her as

I leave the kitchen, her grin turning upside down. The wonderful harmony that we all once had died long ago. When I reach Rosannah's room, I sneak in and rest against the wall opposite her bed. She's asleep on top of the blankets, still dressed in her work clothes from yesterday. I stare at her, mesmerised by how peaceful she looks. I fight the urge to race over to her. I would love to turn her peaceful slumber into screams of terror. The thought makes me smile. At that moment, she stirs awake and sits up, rubbing her eyes. She gasps when she realises someone is in the room with her. I half achieved what I wanted. I watch as her eyes adjust and focus on me. Her expression goes from frightened to annoyed.

"What the hell are you doing in here?" she demands. Where did the fear go? How can she be annoyed at me? I am playing God with her life! The crypt is definitely the place to take her.

"I am taking you out and showing you the grounds. Get ready, you have twenty minutes," I say and rush off leaving her dumbfounded. Downstairs, I bump into Evangeline, who is still here. I am not as annoyed as I should be. The thought of Rosannah not being frightened disturbs me. "I do not think she really believes us," I say staring out of the window with my hands behind my back.

"Why on earth would you think that?" Evangeline asks in her usual dim-witted way. Nicholas pops his head in.

"Who would believe anything he says," he tells Evangeline and disappears before I can grab him. Evangeline giggles lightly. When did the twins get here? I have been so wrapped up with Rosannah that I do not know what is going on in my own house!

"I went to wake her up, and it startled her. When she realised it was me, she got annoyed," I say with a frown. Lawrence pops his head in.

"Well, perving on someone is bound to get their back up," he says with a grin. I am quicker this time. Without looking, I reach out and grab him by the scruff of his shirt. "Erm, this is your shirt," he says quickly. I let go, and he races off. "Can't believe you fell for that!" he yells.

"Ah, that is right, I should have known, judging by the awful pattern on it, that it was not mine. I would not be caught dead in something as hideous as that," I spit. I am met with silence. I smile knowing that it hit home. I turn my attention to Evangeline, who is smiling.

"It's obvious isn't it?" she says tilting her head to the side. "She fancies you." She laughs and walks off. That is not what I want. Terrorized, yes; impressed, yes; infatuated, yes; concupiscent, definitely yes; but fancy? No. I do not want her to fancy me. I sit and read the newspaper to pass some time. Twenty minutes later, I have left the front door wide open and I am leaning against the front of the house, tucked out of the way. After a few minutes of waiting, she walks outside. She stops almost in front of me and closes her eyes, turning her face up to the sun.

"You are late," I say, intentionally startling her. She gathers her composure with a deep breath.

"Sorry, you didn't give me much time to get ready," she complains.

"Never mind, we are heading to the back of the house," I say turning and then walking off leaving her standing there. I walk at a casual pace so she can run after me and catch up.

"Let me guess, we're heading into the crypt, right?" she says with dread. So, she hates the dead? I am worse.

"Yes," I say smiling at her and head to the crypt entrance. Only the entry is visible from up here. It is a doorway with a slope behind it; the rest of the crypt is underground. The doorway is made of stone with a metal barred door. There are five cherubs, three angels, and four vampires carved in the stone above the doorway. My grandfather was a fantasy fan. Rosannah stares at it trying to figure out what is happening in the pictorial. I decide to put her out of her misery. "The angels and cherubs are taking the vampires to heaven," I state, watching her reaction.

"And what is vampire heaven called?" she asks, still staring at the carving.

"Heaven. Follow me," I say opening the door and flicking on a switch just inside. Light cascades down the stairwell. "Close the door behind you," I say over my shoulder as I head down. I hear Rosannah close the door as I reach the bottom. This girl is very slow. I wait for her to reach me. At the bottom of the steep, narrow staircase, a chamber has five aisles branching off it. Each branch shows different carvings of angels and cherubs taking vampires to heaven. It smells of mould and rot down here. I can already see that Rosannah is anxious. Her breathing is uneven and her heart is racing. She is slightly shivering. It is cold and damp down here, but I do not care. "Most of the family down here are Von Smits. Down this aisle are the oldest ones," I say as I point to a branch for Rosannah to lead the way.

Each coffin is sitting peacefully covered in dust on a huge stone shelf. Moss covers the exposed stone. The wooden boxes have decayed somewhat, but the metal boxes inside are still intact. The bodies they house have already decomposed. There are just bones and rags left inside of them. I point to each coffin as we make our way down the aisle. "Here we have Great-great-uncle Mark Von Smit, his wife, Maureen, and their son, David. Then here we have my great-great-grandfather Vernon, and at the end, we have my great-great-grandmother, Vorella. These two are the oldest bodies down here, having died more than five hundred years ago," I say, looking at Rosannah's face. Her nose wrinkles with distaste. I smile inwardly and prod her to go back up the aisle.

"Ow," she says as she jumps.

"Move," I demand.

"Would you be so kind as to move out of the way?" she asks with fake sweetness. I shake my head and point down the aisle. She looks incredulously at me. That is right; you are going to have to squeeze past me. She scowls at me but does as she is told. Trying to keep her warm, little body as far from mine as possible, she passes by me. She does an awful job and her ample bosom slides across me. She looks horrified, but I make no attempt to move. The erection in my jeans is restricting, and I am surprised at how easily she can provoke it. Once out of the aisle, I proceed. "On to the next aisle. Down here, we have my great-great-uncle Mathew and his wife,

June. My great-great-aunt Ethel and her husband,
Joshua." On to the next aisle. Rosannah looks more
and more spooked the further we continue. "Down
this aisle, we have my great-uncle Francis, his wife,
Louisa, and then we have my uncle Frederic, his wife,
Bettie, and my cousin, Ludwig. These last three were
killed when my parents and grandparents were
killed," I say turning to look at Rosannah. She is
looking a shade paler. I relish in disturbing her. On to
the next aisle. "Down this aisle, we have my great-
uncle Julian and his wife, Florence." I grin.

"Why are there only two coffins down this one?"
she asks with narrow eyes.

"Sorry, I do not have enough dead relatives for your
liking," I say quite curt. She blushes, bringing some
colour back to her cheeks. "And now for the last aisle.
Here, we have my grandparents, Raphael and
Evangeline Von Smit," I say proudly.

"So, you and your sister were named after your
grandparents?" she asks. "Yes. My uncle and his wife
had difficulty having children. When my mother had
us, she called my sister and me after her parents.
After Evangeline was born, my uncle's wife fell
pregnant and had a boy, but it was too late to use the
name. Here, we have my mother and father. Elizabeth
and William," I say, pointing to the last two coffins.

"Where are the rest of the families?" Rosannah asks
confused.

"They are not Von Smits and my father's family
have their own vault. We had to fight to have him
here," I say as I shrug my shoulders.

"Seriously, are there really dead bodies in these
boxes?" she asks.

"Yes, I can show you one if you would like. It is no problem opening one of these up," I say hoping she will opt for it. It does nothing to me, but judging by the horror on her face, it would profoundly disturb her.

"Erm, no thank you. I'll just take your word for it," she says hunching her shoulders up. I look down at the emblem on one of the coffins. Each coffin has a heart with a bat on it.

"The Von Smit family emblem," I tell her running my fingers over it. I look at her and catch her staring at me like she is evaluating my face. I suddenly feel uncomfortable. "Time to leave, I think," I say trying to give her a casual smile and shoo her back down the aisle to the staircase.

"So, you're immortal?" she suddenly blurts out over her shoulder.

"Yes," I say deadpan.

"You're as you were all those years ago?" she asks.

"Frozen in time the day I died," I say grimly.

"Who's the eldest vampire you know?" she asks. Why does she keep saying it like that? "Mathias. He's over three thousand years old." I smile. She stops dead at the bottom of the stairs and turns to face me. She bursts out laughing. I have apparently missed the joke.

"That must be why he looks sooo old," she says between laughs. I wait for her to finish.

"He only looks the way he does because he replaced parts of himself. A kind of plastic surgery, if you like. Except he did not go with improvement. He went for downright weird. What makes the whole thing hilarious is that he did all that within his first thousand years. He cannot remember how he looked originally and is doomed to look like a freak forever." I laugh. Rosannah doesn't see the funny side. I realise I have made a grave mistake telling her this particular story. It is not the whole story, but it is enough to have her asking questions. Why did I open my big mouth?

"Can't he just get new body parts and make himself look better?" she asks with confusion. Rosannah has thrown me a lifeline.

"Seriously, have a good think about what you just said," I say raising an eyebrow. I can see the realisation as it hits her. She looks mortified. "Exactly," I say with a smirk. That shut her up and has hopefully stopped her from ever mentioning this again. She stands there for a while, staring into space. I have to put an end to wherever her thoughts might be headed. "Right, now to look at the garden. You first," I say pointing up the stairs.

I am full of bad decisions today, and after five steps, I realise I have made a mistake. I grab her, turn her around, and throw her over my shoulder. Only to a small squeaked protest, must I add. Racing up the remaining stairs, I set her back down on the ground. I watch as she sways on her feet. Surely, that could not have made her dizzy? Once she gets her bearings, I show her around the garden. The garden is expansive, but I only stick to the intricately planted flowerbeds and the water features, which are mainly angels and cherubs. Each water feature has an identical twin except two. They are the only ones that depict vampires. One has a vampire that is dying and an angel carrying him to heaven. The other is God accepting a vampire into heaven. They are situated at the rear of the garden. My grandfather loved all things vampire but kept it hidden.

We work our way through the garden and up to the front gate, which is open. Damn, my siblings. They are lazy, and I am forever closing it and the garage door after them. I hope the open gate is not too tempting to Rosannah. Surely, she wouldn't be stupid enough to try to run off? As we approach the gate, she asks me about the gateposts. Having decided that she wouldn't be stupid enough to try to run, I entertain her question about the plaque and walk over to it. I didn't get to explain what the sign meant before, no thanks to Harry. When my back is turned, that's when she decides to run for it. I let out a huge exasperated growl as she races off like a greyhound chasing a fake rabbit. Except, with Rosannah, the stakes are much higher. She has bolted in the direction of Mr. and Mrs. Grimps' bungalow. An elderly couple who never venture further than their own front door. There's nowhere else for her to run to, but I'll have to get to her before she rings their bell. I'm faster than this girl could ever imagine. With no cars around, I wait for the right moment. Then I make my move.

CHAPTER TEN

Rosannah

We finish in the crypt, and I'm glad, as it creeps me out being down here. Being in such a confined space with all these dead bodies isn't my idea of fun. Raphael has claimed that two of them are his parents, but they can't be. Those two people down here died two hundred and seventy-four years ago. There's just no way his family died when he says they did. And all this about Mathias, that's just absurd! It's all completely unbelievable and yet he fully believes everything he says.

He was so into his storytelling, so animated and full of passion. To him, all of this is real. It's his life and his history, and the more I find out, the more disturbed I am. I remember just staring at his beautiful face feeling incredibly saddened by the madness that has gripped him. I have never met anyone who was insane before and resent the fact that Raphael has to be the first. The depth of his insanity is very alarming. Not just his, but his family's and friend's, too. Raphael must be about twenty-six. He has so much more life ahead of him and yet, so far, he has been dealt such a terrible hand in life. It really is a painful thing to see. My heart actually aches for him, but I have to try to keep my emotions at bay. I wonder what actually happened to his family. Did they abuse him? Are they responsible for his detachment from reality? And what was with him making me pass him so I had no choice but to scrape my breasts against him? Is that how he cops a feel? Raphael breaks me from my thoughts.

"Right, now to look at the garden. You first," he says pointing up the stairs. I take a few steps when suddenly Raphael grabs me, turns me around, and flings me over his shoulder. What the hell is he doing? I go to let out a yelp of shock, but my mouth just won't work properly. I want to scream but what comes out is a small squeak. I feel a force that pushes down on me and the stairs blur in front of my eyes. Before I can focus again, Raphael puts me down on the grass. My head is spinning and I stagger. What did he just do? Did he somehow manage to drug me? How could he have possibly done that? But it's the only explanation. I'm certainly not entertaining the idea Mr. Fruit bat here is a real vampire.

Raphael is in my vision as it comes back to normal. He's looking at me with a puzzled expression. I don't know why you're confused; this is your fault! "Right then, this way," he says, gesturing to a large flowerbed. He has some manners, then? I have to give him that, but that's as far as similarities with regular people go. He has gone too far to be brought back to the world of the sane. I think his parents really do have a lot to answer for. How could they let this happen to all of their children? I know vampires didn't murder them two hundred and seventy-four years ago. They must have abused and abandoned them, and now they're totally messed up, passing this ridiculous story around to try to cover up what actually happened.

I'm better off getting as far away from all of them as possible. I attempt to hatch a plan, but Raphael shows me two very peculiar fountains. "This one is a vampire being carried to heaven and this one is a vampire being accepted into heaven by God. More of my grandfather's decorations. They are the only two that aren't an identical pair." He smiles. Well, it sounds like his grandfather was a big slice of crazy, too. That might explain a few things. We make our way to the front of the garden. I can see that the gate has been left open, surprisingly. I've only ever seen it shut, but then again, how many times have I actually seen it? Never mind. An opportunity has arisen and a plan starts to form in my head. I pretend to listen to what Raphael is saying, but my mind focuses on the gate and my escape. Raphael is so engrossed in showing me all of the many different flowers here that he hasn't realised that freedom is calling me. "These flowers have come from all around the world," he says as we stroll along the front of the garden, his hands behind his back.

"Hmm," I manage to get out as I eye up the gate. My eyes flick to Raphael's legs and feet. They look strong and sturdy. Just how fast can this vampire possibly be? That's if he really even is a vampire. If I leg it and get away from him, I can run down the road to the place I saw next door. Once I get past a certain point, he will have to give up as he might be seen chasing me. I'm pretty fast, and I'm sure I can make it if I catch him off guard. As we approach the gate, I set my plan in motion. "So, what's the history of that sign on the gate over there?" Raphael gets distracted, and he walks away from me towards the column on the right. Very Stupid, vampire boy. I seize my opportunity; it's now or never. I pelt it. I hear an exasperated growl from him as I speed away. I run as fast as I can, and I'm amazed that I can't hear him following me.

I see the gap in the trees ahead and push myself on. I risk a glance back and feel so relieved that Raphael is nowhere in sight. He must have realised it would be a stupid idea to chase after me out onto the road. Running after me and trying to drag me away in front of his neighbours might be a bit too much for him. So, his madness knows some bounds, after all. Good, that works in my favour. I eventually reach the garden gate and barge it open. I have the front door in my sights, and I know I've made it. I'm so happy to see the lights are on. Someone is home. I race down the garden path and reach out for the bell as I approach the front door. Just as my outstretched finger is about to push it, a gust of wind whips around me, and Raphael appears in front of me. A mixture of emotion whirs through me as he grabs my outstretched arm and pulls me to him, his body absorbing my momentum.

"I don't think so," he whispers into my ear. What the hell just happened? I left him standing behind like an idiot—there's no way he could have caught up with me! Maybe he used a hidden path? Even if there was one, he would have had to run down his garden and then across. It would be practically the same distance I just ran and I would have seen him move around or across me! He wraps me up into his chest, and we suddenly move incredibly fast. This time, I close my eyes to avoid any dizziness. Before I know it, he's plonking me back onto my bed and I open my eyes in amazement.

"Why did you do that?" he growls at me.

"How the hell did you do that?" I ask incredulously, jumping off the bed to stand in front of him. "How can you be that fast? It isn't possible," I demand. He's suddenly inches from my face.

"Let me give you an idea of how fast I am. I stood where you left me until you reached out for the bell. That's when I started to run after you," he strains through gritted teeth. No way, there's just no way!

"You're honestly trying to tell me that you ran that fast?" I ask staring him up and down.

"Yes," he growls. Then it really hits me. He's been telling me the truth, they all have! All those times I thought I was going mad or had been drugged seeing them flash around, they were actually moving that fast! Their eyes really are light grey, and they really were drinking blood!

"Oh, my God, you really are a vampire, aren't you?" I ask in shock. He raises his eyebrows at me. So, he's not a nutjob. That's great, but he's a goddamn vampire instead. Is that any better? "It was one thing when I thought you were a nutjob but a vampire? I can't believe they exist. Why the hell do you have to be one?" I ask, frowning. He says nothing. "That has to be the most disturbing thing I have ever come across!" I shout, shaking my head. His face softens and then frowns.

"Why did you run, Rosannah?" he asks calmly.

"What the hell did you expect? Trap a girl here, tell her your crazy stories and introduce her to your crazy family and friends! I thought it was the ramblings of mad people. Of course, I was going to bolt the first opportunity I got!" I say incredulously. His eyes are suddenly black like onyx, and I can see that he's incredibly angry, but there's a look in there that I've never seen before. His lips twitch, and in an instant, he grabs the shoulders of my cardigan. He wraps his fingers in the material so tight it causes it to tear. I can feel the material burn my skin, ow! I stare into the bottomless pits of his eyes, too petrified to look away.

He doesn't say a word but lunges for my throat. I feel his cold lips on my neck and then two very sharp teeth pierce my skin. They sink deep into the flesh. Panic sets in and I can barely breathe. Taking in shallow, quick breaths, I stare at the ceiling. The agony of Raphael's bite overtakes the pain from the chaffing of my cardigan. It spreads through the muscles in my neck like a multitude of wasp stings. I nearly pass out but somehow manage to cling on to consciousness. I instinctively reach up and push on his chest with strength I never knew existed. I try to get away from him, but it isn't enough. In a flash, he releases my cardigan and grabs the back of my neck and waist for better leverage, pulling me tighter and trapping my hands between our chests. This forces my head backwards and I close my eyes as he pulls his teeth out of my flesh.

He clamps down with his mouth, sucking the blood from my wound. I can feel his throat muscles contract against my collarbone as he swallows my blood. A trail of warm liquid runs down my neck and makes its way to my breasts. The only sound I can hear is my breathing, but I can feel the vibration of him lightly growling through his chest. After a few mouthfuls, he lets me go. Grabbing at the bed on my way down, I crumple into a heap at his feet. I stare up his body to see his face. He kneels down in front of me, his eyes still black. They flick down at my breasts, and with one cold hand, he pushes my head back. Pulling my vest down slightly, he laps up the blood trail from the top of my cleavage up to the wound on my neck. I feel fire rush through my body, and I gasp at how soft and cool his tongue feels running along my skin.

"Real enough for you?" he whispers in my ear. I nod, unable to say anything. "Good. I've only just got started," he sneers at me. Then he's gone. I sit on the floor for goodness knows how long trying to get myself back together. Once I come back to my senses, I rush to the bathroom and stare at myself in the mirror. I can see the blood on my top and the tears in my cardigan. I take it off and see the burns on my skin, but when I look at my neck, there's nothing there. No trace of blood, no bruising, no wounds, nothing! I touch where he bit me and instantly feel the fire race through my body again. What am I? Horny?

I drop my hand quickly as if the sensation scalded me and I suddenly feel dirty. The need to wash and put fresh clothes on is so great that I dash into the shower as fast as I can. Once I clean up, I can think straight. I remember that vampire laws, laws he governs, will protect me. Why would he break the rules? Did he think I wouldn't tell? I'm broken from my thoughts by the sound of chattering in the distance. I head to the door and try the handle. I'm surprised when it turns and the door opens. I creep out into the hall and look at the front door. Raphael is talking to some visitors. I can't quite see them, but it looks like two females. My attention turns back to Raphael. I stare at his broad back. He's quite the man.

Well, you know what I mean. Strong and powerful. There's no escaping a male like him. That burning feeling races through me. Damn, what is wrong with me?

"She was a lovely girl; it was quite a pleasure to show her my home," Raphael says, turning on the charm. I don't stand a chance of getting down there. I go into the music room and look through the window instead. I'm so happy to see Brianna and Marie. I can just about see them from here. I knew someone would come looking for me. Well, my mother wouldn't, but Brianna definitely would. She wants her picture and that's at all costs. Now that she's seen Raphael in the flesh, she doesn't need it anymore. I smile at the thought. Wait! What are you thinking? Try to get their attention, you bloody fool! I start waving my arms around like I'm on fire and banging on the glass. They should be able to hear me, but they don't look up, they completely ignore me. They must be brainwashed by Raphael. I stop and rest my forehead on the glass. He hands Brianna a key. It must be so she can feed Marmalade. Although I'd love to go home, I'm not as upset as I should be. I should be desperate to get away from Raphael, but something keeps drawing me in.

CHAPTER ELEVEN

Raphael

That girl drives me crazy! I wanted to break her in a controlled manner, but I no longer think that is possible. Her anger ignited me and sent me over the edge. Now I have tasted her blood. Ah, how sweet and salty, metallic and warm it is. It's the best thing I have ever tasted, followed closely by her skin. When I licked her breast, her skin was so soft and supple. Succulent and delicious. And her little gasps? Gah! It was beyond a turn on, and I'm still hard! I didn't know she would excite me this much! It took all I had in me to walk away and not take her there on the floor. But now that I've crossed the line, I won't be able to stop myself from biting her again and again and again. Will I even be able to keep it just to biting her? I am not sure.

What is this? There is a rumble outside. A vehicle driving toward the house. Now is not the time for visitors. I race out of my bedroom and downstairs. Closing my eyes, I listen to the world outside. The vehicle has now stopped and slow footsteps are making their way to my front door. Great, humans. How did they get in? The blasted gate is still open! I can tell by the idle chitchat and whiny voices that it's 'sack of potatoes' and 'easy to brainwash.' I open the front door before they can knock. I don't want Rosannah to know they are here, but with their big mouths, she will most certainly hear them. "Ah,

Marie, what a pleasant surprise. How can I help you fine ladies on this wonderful sunny morning?" I say, putting on my best dazzling smile. There's no point in brainwashing them until I have to.

"Rosannah was right; you are completely gorgeous!" sack of potatoes gushes. Easy to brainwash jabs her in the ribs. She smiles apologetically but looks mortified. Rosannah thinks I'm gorgeous? Interesting.

"This is Brianna. She's also from Tilberry Sales. We're terribly sorry to disturb you, Mr. Monstrum. We were just wondering if you knew where Rosannah might be?" asks easy to brainwash. Brianna? Well, now I have a name for a face I wish never to see again.

"She turned up, I showed her the garden and crypt, and then she was on her way. Perhaps she's just at home," I say with a smile.

"The problem is that she was due back at work and hasn't turned up. She hasn't phoned anyone and no one knows where she is. It is very, very uncharacteristic of her. Brianna, here, lives a floor below her and has been knocking on her door. Looking through the letterbox, the post is on the floor and poor Marmalade has just been meowing her head off. No one is feeding the poor thing. Something is very wrong. Our next course of action is the police," easy to brainwash says glumly. Flicking my eyes from one to the other, I stare deep into the both of their eyes.

"You will not look at the window above. There is no one there. In fact, no one is here but me. Rosannah went travelling around the world, you have just forgotten even though she has talked about it non-stop for the past month. She's away for at least twelve months and will be in contact then," I say brainwashing them. Right then, Rosannah stops banging on the window and the smile that spreads across my face is mirrored by the two idiots in front of me. "Stop that!" I growl. Their grins drop. "She was a lovely girl, it was quite a pleasure to show her my home," I say smiling at them. I reach into my coat pocket and hand the dumpy one a key. I had Evangeline get one cut as I was planning to sort out this cat of Rosannah's, but an opportunity has just presented itself to me. "Feed the cat regularly, Brianna, until Rosannah returns. She had asked you before she left," I say.

"Yes," she replies. I shut the door in their faces. I'm still furious and head into the TV room.

"Ah, so someone sunk their teeth into our little guest," smirks Lawrence.

"I forgot you lot were here," I say begrudgingly.

"You know what, Raphael, just get it over and done with," says Nicholas.

"What?" I ask, irritated.

"Just bang her and get it over with," Lawrence says casually. I glare at him. "Fair enough." He shrugs.

"Know what you need? A trip to the local prison, I think a killing spree is in order." Nicholas smiles.

"You're right, that's exactly what I need. I'll meet you there." I race off and hear Nicholas and Lawrence follow me. Tonight, I'm going to be a convict's worst nightmare!

CHAPTER TWELVE

Rosannah

Trying to get Brianna and Marie's attention was tiring. After a long nap, I go downstairs and come across an amused Lawrence. This is nothing new. He's always smirking about something or the other. A filthy mind and always up to no good. "What's got you so happy?" I ask him suspiciously.

"We went on a bender." He grins. A bender? I thought they could only have blood?

"Who is we and what would a vampire bender entail?" I ask, intrigued.

"Raphael, Nicholas, and myself. We left Evangeline at home. I guess you could say it was a lads' night out. During a vampire bender, you drain as many people dry as possible in a set amount of time. We drained twenty-three collectively in twenty minutes. Raphael scored the most, as usual. He's faster than we are. Well, you should know," he smirks. I suddenly feel sick.

"You killed all those people?" I ask, horrified.

"Of course, we all did. But only criminals, they're the most fun. They put up the best fight," he says, his eyes shining with excitement. Criminals or not, they're not the law! Well, not human law anyway! I just stare at him. "Ah, your face, look how horrified you are." He laughs. He thinks everything is one big joke. I stomp off up the stairs, leaving him standing there chuckling. I'm truly appalled. I go to Raphael's room and knock on the door. I won't lose my manners. He opens the door and leans on the frame with his right arm, blocking the view of his room with his body. What his room looks like isn't important; I just want to give him a piece of my mind. Keep telling yourself that. I walk under his left arm, which is still holding the door, and into his room. The Dracula room. I stop just before the bed. I can't help but stare at it. It's magnificent. It's a beautifully carved, oak four-poster bed draped in black silk.

"Come in," Raphael says sarcastically, still at the door. I turn to face him with my arms crossed.

"How could you kill all those people?" I ask, disgusted.

"It's pretty easy. Break some necks; rip a few bodies apart with my bare hands," he says indifferently as he swaggers over to me. This winds me up even more.

"It's so wrong; you're not the law," I scathe.

"Oh, I beg to differ," he smirks, moving closer. His eyes take on a slightly darker shade, and my confidence falters.

"You're wrong, and you shouldn't do it. You're not above the law, the human law," I whisper. He stops right in front of me.

"I'm a vampire, it's what I do. I feed, I torture, and I kill. Don't talk about things you know nothing about," he whispers sarcastically back. I look at his features. He has such an angelic face. I really don't want to see him as a complete monster. I just can't justify liking him in any way. I feel ashamed for even finding him remotely attractive. Anger builds up in me at how cruel life can be.

"It's disgusting," I yell in his face. His eyes turn completely black in an instance, and he grabs my butt pulling me into him, pressing a very hard erection into me.

Leaning very close to my ear, he whispers, "Quite a fiery temper, you know just how to push my buttons to get me really going. If you had been like this from the beginning, things certainly would have been different by now." Lust douses his words, and I'm horrified. We were just talking about killing people, and he manages to fit in getting horny? He leans back to gauge the expression on my face. I have the perfect shot, and so I slap him full force across the face. The sting spreads across the palm of my hand, and I wince. I know for him it didn't hurt, but I wanted to offend him. I think it worked because he doesn't look too impressed.

"What the hell makes you think I'd be remotely interested in you?" I scathe trying to squirm free. His grip tightens. He looks furious, but I remember there isn't a whole lot he can do about it. He completely caught me off guard when he bit me before, but I know my rights and I'm going to flaunt them. "You can't hurt me because of your laws, remember?" I say. He smirks at me. He thinks this is funny? I decide to try my luck even more. "You're a hideous monster that I wouldn't touch in a million years! I'd say that men like you should get locked up for the things you've done, but you're not even a..." I don't get to finish my sentence. He lunges at my throat again sinking his fangs into my flesh. He's much faster, wasting no time to suck my blood. Just a few mouthfuls and he licks the wound clean. The same fire burns its way through my body like last time. He lets go of me, but I manage to stay standing this time. I look into his eyes, and he's certainly not sorry about anything he's done. No remorse whatsoever. "You bit me again and you're not allowed to!" I state shocked that he's broken the rules, again. He smiles sweetly at me.

"Honey, the law states you can't be killed unless you're a convicted criminal. And it also says you can't be changed unless it's approved by The Synod. It protects you to a certain extent, but what it does not protect you from is being bitten. And it certainly doesn't protect you from me. I govern the law; do you think I'm going to punish myself?" He looks me up and down and leans closer to my ear. "I can do whatever I like with you. You shouldn't have shown me just how feisty you are." He pulls back and smiles at my horrified expression. I run past him and back towards my room, bumping into Evangeline on my way. She is carrying a plate of food.

"Whoa, you're in a hurry." She smiles at me. I grab her hand and try to pull her towards my room. She's like a solid concrete block! She gets the hint straight away and pulls me there instead, slamming the door behind her. "Oh, so what's the dishy gossip?" she asks. She can barely contain her excitement as she places the plate on the bedside table.

"I'm really scared of your brother," I confide in her quietly. She scrunches up her face.

"Why would you be scared of him?" She looks so confused.

"Well, he keeps...biting me, and I think he wants to...do things to me" His sentence fills my mind making me feel incredibly embarrassed. She smiles at me.

"Well, of course, he does. You're pretty hot, and he is a male, plus he's a vampire. Biting you was inevitable," she chirps. I wanted her to be on my side. I'm a virgin, and I don't want to offer that up on a plate to him. He shouldn't just take it either. But there's a part of me that does want him to and that frightens me the most. I debate about telling her my real reasons I'm frightened and decide to.

"Well, the problem is—" I glance at her to see that she's looking behind me. I know Raphael is there. How did I not hear the door open? Oh, yes, that's right. They're masters of creep here! I stop talking and don't turn around to see if it's him.

"Don't worry, it'll all be fine," she says as she whizzes past me. The door shuts and locks. Ah, my newfound freedom has been cut short. I eat what she left for me and decide to head to bed. Being left to my own thoughts, my mind starts whirring. So, he can do whatever he likes to me, and I can't stop him? That's a terrible thing, especially when there's a part of me that actually wants him to. I have to resist as best I can. I'm strong enough to do this. I think.

CHAPTER THIRTEEN

Raphael

Lying back on my bed, hands behind my head, I smile at the conversation Lawrence has just had with Rosannah. Footsteps and Heartbeats make their way to my bedroom. An impatient knock on the door. I whisk over and open it to reveal an irate Rosannah. Eyebrows slanted and cheeks an angry rouge, she bypasses my arm to enter into my room. She walks over to my bed, where I had just been laying a few minutes ago, and stares at it. That's right, take it in. I'll hold you down and fuck you in it if you're lucky. "Come in," I say sarcastically. She turns with her arms crossed. Oh, this is going to be amusing.

"How could you kill all those people?" she asks with horror. This girl is too fastidious.

"It's pretty easy. Break some necks; rip a few bodies apart with my bare hands," I say as I saunter over to her. Her heart beats faster.

"It's so wrong, you're not the law," she spits.

"Oh, I beg to differ," I contradict and watch as her anger dissolves.

"You're wrong, and you shouldn't do it. You're not above the law, the human law." Her voice is small and weak. I close the gap between us with one final step.

"I'm a vampire, it's what I do. I feed, I torture, and I kill. Don't talk about things you know nothing about." I match her whisper but with a bite of sarcasm. Her face softens, and her eyes dart across my face. What is she looking for?

"It's disgusting," she suddenly shouts. Her rage is like a switch and has me rock hard for her. I grab her by the ass and pull her into me. Barely containing myself, I whisper the truth.

"Quite a fiery temper, you know just how to push my buttons to get me really going. If you had been like this from the beginning, things certainly would have been different by now." I force myself to pull back. I watch as Rosannah, in typical human fashion, pulls her arm back and swings elbow first for my face. I have plenty of opportunities to stop her, but I let her have her best shot. It's a dangerous move, but I'm already playing it. Her hand connects with my left cheek. Her fingers splay and her eyes close as the impact tremors along her arm. When she opens her eyes again, I watch the pain register and she grimaces. It hurt her way more than it could ever hurt me. I know I shouldn't have done it, but I had to see it play out. Now I know.

"What the hell makes you think I'd be remotely interested in you?" she spits with venom. She starts to wriggle free. I gradually tighten my grip until she stops. "You can't hurt me because of your laws remember?" she says. She thinks she knows it all. "You're a hideous monster that I wouldn't touch in a million years! I'd say that men like you should get locked up for the things you've done, but you're not even a..." I zone out halfway through, seeing red. When I come to, I'm sucking blood from her neck. I lick the wounds, sealing them off. What have I done? You've gone beyond your boundaries. You can't let any emotion play ball. Stick to the void. I release her, and she looks as shocked as I feel, but I push the feeling away. "You bit me again, and you're not allowed to!" she says. I know I have no intention of stopping. I smile at her. She thinks she has this all sussed out.

"Honey, the law states you can't be killed unless you're a convicted criminal. And it also states you can't be changed unless it's approved by The Synod. It protects you to a certain extent, but what it does not protect you from is being bitten. And it certainly doesn't protect you from me. I govern the law; do you think I'm going to punish myself?" I look her up and down. She's in so much trouble, and she has no idea. I take all her curves in and leaning forward, I whisper in her ear, "I can do whatever I like to you, and you can't stop me." I pull back. She looks truly horrified. I can't help but smile as she runs past me and out of my room.

"Whoa, you're in a hurry," I hear Evangeline say. She's bringing up some of Lawrence's cuisine, no doubt. I hear them both scuttle into Rosannah's room and close the door. I head out of my room and stand outside listening. "Oh, so what's the dishy gossip?" Evangeline asks. She knows exactly what it is. She would have heard everything.

"I'm really scared of your brother," Rosannah whispers. It was about time she was scared of me!

"Why would you be afraid of him?" asks a confused Evangeline. She's caught in my web, and I do not intend to let her go. Maybe that's why she should be scared?

"Well, he keeps...biting me, and I think he wants to...do things to me" If you only knew the half of it. *The things I could do to you, which gives me an idea. The next time I bite her, I will try to project into her mind, like a vision. We vampires have many abilities, all to aid feeding. Not that we need any help—we have our brute strength—but to be able to feed and blend in, we have to use trickery of the mind. Hopefully, Rosannah is only immune to the brainwashing.*

"Well, of course, he does. You're pretty hot, and he is a male, plus he's a vampire. Biting you was inevitable," Evangeline says. *She has some sense then, praise the Lord!*

"What are you doing?" whispers Lawrence, who has made his way next to me. I signal to him to be quiet.

"Well, the problem is..." Rosannah cuts off and her heart rate picks up. *Great.*

"Thanks, bro," I whisper sarcastically.

"No problem. Anytime you want your plans ruined, call me," he whispers back, waggling a phone gesture at me. I give him an unimpressed smile as he slinks away.

"Don't worry, it'll all be fine," says Evangeline as she races out of the room, locking the door behind her. I only get a look at Rosannah's back. I motion for Evangeline to be quiet, and we race into the kitchen. "What's going on?" she asks.

"He was eavesdropping," says Lawrence as he enters the room.

"That's incredibly rude," says Evangeline, putting her hands on her hips.

"I'm surprised you don't carry a big wooden spoon around with you for all the stirring you do!" I glare at Lawrence, who smirks in reply. I turn back to Evangeline. "Don't act like you didn't eavesdrop on us in my room!" I say watching Evangeline's stern look melt away into a pout. "Anyway, we need to go and get supplies. Rosannah is locked in her room, she'll be safe while we go and get our usual. Agreed?" I ask.

"Didn't you three go out on a bender?" asks a confused Evangeline.

"Yes, but I am low on stock in the house," I say with irritation.

"Oh, well, let's go then." She smiles. Lawrence just nods.

"I'll meet you all at the hospital." I race off. I always go ahead as my siblings wouldn't get anywhere. I've brainwashed everyone there so no one knows they exist. They'd just be ignored. Within in minutes, I'm there. "Hey, Bill," I greet the security guard.

"The usual?" he asks.

"Yes, please." I smile.

"Let me just put the loop on." He smiles as he presses a button on the CCTV machine. It's funny. Bill has no idea what the usual involves. He's just brainwashed into running a pre-recorded loop on the CCTV and then to give me the key to the blood supply. Once I'm gone, he is brainwashed into forgetting all about me. My greeting triggers it all. Breaking in would be suspicious and a security guard claiming he saw nothing wouldn't go down too well, either. Some missing blood bags and the hospital will assume they've been misplaced or used without being documented. "Here's the key." Bill smiles at me as he hands it over. I hear the others coming and they're by my side within seconds. I suddenly get an odd feeling. Something doesn't feel right.

"Are you okay, Raph?" Evangeline asks.

"What?" I ask as I come out of my daze.

"You look like something is wrong," she points out with concern.

"Something is not right. I think we need to head back," I say. Nicholas huffs and Evangeline pouts.

"Do we really have to head back? There's nothing wrong. You're just paranoid," says Lawrence. I turn to Bill and hand the key back to him.

"You will only remember me when I turn up here again for the usual. If anyone asks, you had an uneventful night tonight. You drank too much coffee and had to pee a lot," I say to him.

"Yes," he replies.

"Since when am I ever paranoid?" I ask Lawrence and race off without even checking to see if the others are following me. When I reach the house, I can smell a new scent that I don't recognise. The others appear by my side.

"Okay, so it looks like we have a new visitor," Lawrence says.

"A human, a foolish human," I growl.

"Check the grounds in case anyone else has tried their luck," I tell Evangeline. She dashes off while the rest of us quietly race in and follow the new scent. Looking at each other, we stand outside Rosannah's door.

CHAPTER FOURTEEN

Rosannah

I'm awoken from my sleep by a creaking floorboard. Damn you, Raphael! Sneaking in my room again! I open my eyes and sit up straight. I see a dark figure hidden by the shadows in the far corner of the room. Hold on, the floorboard creaked. Honestly, can I put it past Raphael to play tricks on me? No, plus there's no way anyone or anything could sneak in here without him knowing. I relax with a huge sigh.

"Raphael, this is no time to be playing tricks on me!" I whisper angrily. There's no response. What's he playing at? "Raphael, I know you're there. I know that only you would creep into my room to torture me more than you already have," I say as the dark figure shifts slightly. "Raphael, stop being so stupid and come out into the light so I can see you!" I demand. The figure steps forward into a pool of moonlight streaming in through the window. It highlights their face, and I can see straight away that it's not Raphael. I should be incredibly frightened, but for some bizarre reason, I'm not. I feel so drawn to him like I would follow him to the ends of the earth and back. He's ruggedly handsome with cropped blond hair and piercing green eyes. His cheekbones sit high and his jaw is shadowed with stubble. I'm completely mesmerised. I don't understand why I'm so attracted

118

to him. He's nowhere near as gorgeous as Raphael, and yet, I feel the pull of him. He holds out a hand to reveal an acorn. I look down at it confused. Why on earth is he showing me that?

"Don't worry," he whispers, looking slightly worried. Suddenly, he throws the acorn at me, and it hits me straight in the forehead.

"Ow, what the hell was that for?" I yell, rubbing my head with my hand, trying to ease the pain. He walks confidently over to me.

"Sorry about that. I had to be sure they hadn't changed you. If you were changed you would have caught and crushed that acorn," he says as he bends down and collects it from the floor. Throwing it in the air, he catches it and pockets it as he stands.

"So, instead, you decided to crush it on my forehead?" I ask sarcastically. "Well, I'm certainly not one of them. What are you doing here?" I ask him as he sits next to me on the bed, looking at my forehead. He then focuses on my eyes. I can see that he's as mesmerised by me as I am of him. What is this all about?

"My name is Alex. Now I can see you don't have those grey eyes. I'm here to rescue you," he says, his eyes fixed on mine.

"Why?" is all I can manage with those deep green pools in front of me.

"You see, I'm part of a group that spends its time hunting down missing people who have been kidnapped by vampires. We use magic spells to help locate vampires and their captives. You should feel a pull towards me," he says with a smile. So, that's why I'm drawn to him, I'm not attracted to him, it's just a spell! That's a relief. I was beginning to think I was starting to fall for anyone. It's still just Raphael, then. So, magic exists? Well, I shouldn't be surprised anymore.

"Well, you should have known I wasn't a vampire then if you can locate them," I say with a huff.

"You could have been turned by the time I got here," he says with a grim smile.

"Isn't that a process that takes a while?" I ask suspiciously.

"I have no idea how old the vampires are that live here, but I have to think the worst-case scenario. You see, the older the vampire, the faster the change. Now, let's get you out of here," he says with a grin. Suddenly, the pull is gone and a terrible thought occurs to me. The thought of walking out of here and never seeing Raphael again creates a painful divide in me that I cannot bear. I tried to run when I thought he was mad, and I didn't have a lot of feelings for him, but now I can't think of anything that would make me leave him.

"I can't leave," I murmur out loud. Alex's face goes from shock to confusion, to determination. He pulls the covers off me and leans closer, forcing me back onto my elbows. He continues until he ends up on his hands and knees above me. Still working that spell are we?

"Damn it," he mutters. "You don't want to be one, do you?" he asks slightly peeved.

"No, why would I want to be one?" I ask.

"You'd be surprised," he murmurs to himself. There are people out there who actually want to be vampires? That's...disturbing. Alex looks deep into my eyes again. "You want to leave," he says.

"Well, I'd rather you weren't right on top of me, but there you are," I say sarcastically. He looks down at our bodies and then up at me and smiles apologetically. "You only have the opportunity to go now. Once they know I've been here, they won't leave you on your own again," he says hurriedly.

"I'm on my own?" I ask incredulously.

"Yes, they've all gone to get blood. They have to get it somehow. Haven't you paid any attention to them?" he says looking into my eyes intently again. Well, I've paid attention to one of them.

"Three of them went drinking the other night; they shouldn't need to get supplies." I shrug.

He pulls a look of disgust, which then turns into a slight panic. "Look, I'm sorry to push you here, but they could be back at any minute. They may already know I'm here. We've got to leave now," he says in a rush. Should I go? On the one hand, I should leave for obvious reasons, but on the other, I just couldn't face leaving Raphael. That makes me one of the most stupid people on the planet. Alex leans closer. "I honestly don't know why you can't make up your mind. You should be jumping at the chance to be rescued, and yet, you want to stay here!" he yells. I just stay put, staring at him. He must think that I'm completely nuts. Well, I am. "Why don't you want to leave? Why on earth would you want to stay here with them?" he asks. Clunk, creak. We both look over at the door as it slowly reveals a bewildered Raphael flanked by the twins. He takes the scene in and anger flashes across his face.

"Oh my, that's an interesting position you've gotten yourself into, Rosannah," says an amused Lawrence.

"It's not what it looks like," I say, feeling panicked.

"Really? Because I could have sworn it looks like...hey!" Nicholas shoves a laughing Lawrence. Thank goodness. Alex and I then eye each other, and that's when I realise I'm in just a vest and panties. I can now see just how bad it looks. He jumps up to stand between my legs, and I sit up.

"Great, now this looks even worse!" I yell at his crotch.

"Doesn't look too bad from where I'm standing." Alex grins. I let out a little laugh, but a deep growl cuts me off. Raphael. Alex then looks serious. He'd forgotten that he's been caught. In a flash, Raphael has him by the scruff of the neck at the door and the twins are holding each of my arms. I look from one to the other. Why the hell are they holding me? Alex starts to choke as Raphael tightens his grip on his collar.

"Don't hurt him; he was only trying to save me!" I yelp, trying to run to his aid, but four solid arms stop me. Ah, now I see. They must have expected this reaction from Raphael. I don't understand why it would bother him if I left anyway. It would certainly pain me, but it shouldn't affect him at all. Unless, I'm his play toy and he'll have nothing to torment anymore. But, surely there are plenty of girls that he could have as play toys? Actually, scrap that thought. I look at a bright red Alex. "Stop it, you're killing him!" I yell at Raphael. He sneers in disgust and then nods at the twins. In a flash, they all exit the room, locking the door behind them. With the twins gone, the force of me trying to get to Alex is unleashed, and I flop face first onto the bed. I shove myself up onto my hands and sit back, leaning against the headboard wondering what I can do to help Alex. Evangeline will surely help. I wonder where she is.

CHAPTER FIFTEEN

Raphael

"Why don't you want to leave? Why on earth would you want to stay here with them?" a male voice yells. I open the door, and we rushed in. I look on in confusion as I see Rosannah propped up on her elbows lying on the bed with a man I have never seen before on top of her. She's in nothing but a vest and panties. Suddenly, rage fills me.

"Oh my, that's an interesting position you've gotten yourself into," pipes up Lawrence.

"It's not what it looks like!" protests Rosannah. It sure as hell better not be!

"Really? Could have sworn it looks like...hey!" Luckily for Lawrence, Nicholas stopped him mid-sentence. Rosannah and this male look at each other and then look alarmed. They try to get out of their compromising position, but she ends up sat up with him standing between her legs, dick in her face.

"Great, now this looks even worse!" she cries.

"Doesn't look too bad from where I'm standing," the male smirks. A growl leaves my throat and the male stops. That wiped the smile off his face.

"Stop her," I whisper to the twins as I race over, grab the man by the scruff of the neck, and get back to the doorway. Rosannah looks confused. You'll understand soon enough. Looking at the male, I feel pure contempt. I tighten my grip on his collar, and he begins to choke and splutter.

"Don't hurt him; he was only trying to save me!" cries Rosannah as she tries to leap forward. The twins hold her back with ease, and I can see that it has dawned on her why they are there. I keep my grip on the male's collar, and he begins to stop struggling. "Stop it, you're killing him!" Rosannah cries. How pathetic, she wants to save this waste of space. It's guys like him who threaten our secrecy. I sneer in disgust and nod at the twins to release her and come with me. The twins obey and after the door locks behind us, I hear her flop onto the bed. Followed by the twins, I whisk the male down into the dining room where Evangeline is waiting. She shakes her head, indicating to me that there's no trace of anyone else around. She then pulls out a chair and I let the male flop lifelessly into it. I look at him with disgust. I have no idea why he is here, but I am not happy about it. Why he was on top of her? Was he trying to seduce her? The thought that she could ever actually be attracted to him makes me feel sick. I can hear Rosannah calling Evangeline.

"You're not to go to her," I order. She nods. Once the male wakes up, the torture can begin. After two hours, the most we can get out of him is that his name is Alex and he's here to rescue Rosannah. He doesn't know who he works for or how he came to know that Rosannah is here. He can't even tell us how he knows about vampires. He's pretty beaten up by the time I finish asking him questions, but for the fun of it, I break his wrist and watch him scream in agony. It's the loudest I've gotten out of him so far. I then watch his eyes fade as he passes out from the pain. "Stay here with him. I'm going to see Rosannah," I tell the others, who nod before feeding from him.

CHAPTER SIXTEEN

Rosannah

I tried calling Evangeline, tiny whispers at first, then yelling and screaming, but all I got in response was complete silence. I figured that she wasn't coming, so I gave up. Then the screams started. To begin with, they came in waves, but over time, they have gotten louder and louder. Like a tide that comes in gradually, turning into tidal waves, bashing the shoreline with each stroke. Each one cuts right into the very soul of me. I cringe at every scream and work my way down the bed until I'm lying flat on my back, staring at the ceiling. I resort to biting my hand to keep from screaming. It's painful but effective.

"ARGHHH!" I suck in another hiss and bite down on my red raw hand. Then there's nothing but silence. Eerie silence. Alex must have given up and died! Clunk. My heart sinks into my stomach, and I stare at the ceiling, wide-eyed, and let my hand drop. I know it's Raphael. I sit up and scramble back against the headrest, wanting to be as far away from him as possible. He's standing by the door, blood splatter on his exposed skin. A bright cherry red glistens around his mouth. Alex's blood! He slowly wipes it away with his black shirtsleeve, keeping his eyes fixed on mine. His face is back to being perfect again. Angelic, like butter wouldn't melt, but I know different. He appears as if nothing has happened—only the blood that stains his pale hands and neck betrays him. It displays the monster that he truly is. I stare, my eyes unable to look away, afraid to do or say anything. He has those cloudy black eyes that I've seen before. And those eyes have led to me being bitten. Suddenly, he's right next to the bed, and I throw my good hand over my mouth to stifle a yelp. My heart is pounding, having lodged itself in my throat. Raphael bends his knees to lower himself to my height and stares into my eyes.

"You see, Rosannah, I have a problem. I have a man downstairs who has so far been of no help to me. How do you suggest I end his miserable life?" he says slowly, with feigned care. He's still alive, after all that screaming? "I mean, you looked quite close to him, seems only right that you should be the one who decides his demise," he says, while he trails a finger along the bed right next to my bare left leg. His words are like ice, trickling down my spine.

"You don't have to kill him. He hasn't done anything wrong," I say, shaking my head.

"He has done more wrong than you could ever know!" he yells at me, causing me to jump, again. "Besides, as far as I'm concerned, he's a liability I don't want hanging around. I am within perfect rights to execute him," he sneers at me, leaning so close he's just millimetres from my cheek.

"He came here to rescue me; I will tell The Synod that," I say, crossing my arms and staring straight ahead.

"You're so sure that he was telling you the truth. Do you really believe everything you're told?" he whispers, his eyes boring into the side of my face. Deep down, I know Alex is a good man—I can feel it.

"You can't kill him," I say, my voice barely a whisper. My eyes flick to his mouth as it twitches. He scrunches up his lips, trying to hide his anger.

"You like him," he sneers.

"What? Don't be so ridiculous! How could I possibly like him? I don't even know him!" I say incredulously. Turning to look at him, I put us nose to nose, but I don't care. This strangely reminds me of the kind of conversations I have with my mother. She's just as preposterous.

"You two looked close enough," he says with disgust, leaning back to look me up and down.

"That was him working some locator spell that made me want to follow him. It helps with the rescuing process. The seeker wants to find the captive; the captive wants to find the seeker," I say with a shrug.

"In all of my years, I have never heard of such a thing. I can safely say that he was lying," he says. Lying? But I felt the pull! The anger falls off of his face and a blank expression replaces it. His eyes transform back to their normal light grey and he stands back up.

"You didn't go with him, did you?" he asks deadpan.

"No," I say, reluctantly. "But I felt a pull. I've never felt anything like it. It was rather peculiar," I say, trying to look unfazed. It's the truth, well half of it. Something flashes very quickly across his face and in the blink of an eye, he's on the bed, crouching with a leg on either side of mine.

"If it was that strong, why didn't you leave?" he asks, staring deep into my eyes. He's searching for something. "The other day you couldn't get away fast enough but now..." He leaves the sentence hanging there. I try to keep my eyes on his.

"I know I won't get far from you," I say watching his eyes as they dart about my face, trying my best not to get dizzy. Technically, I'm not lying. There's no way we'd have gotten very far without Raphael catching up to us, but that's not the reason I didn't go. I get the feeling he knows this and is playing games with me. What's Raphael's favourite pastime? Torturing by any means possible and I get to be the live-in victim. How joyous. His mouth curves up in a half smile.

"This is true but you could have told him that," he says playfully as he leans forward like he's going to kiss me. He lightly falls onto his hands and my heart races. I stare helplessly as he moves so close, his mouth right against my neck. I suck in a deep breath and hold it, anticipating a bite. "Why didn't you answer his question?" he whispers, rubbing his lips up and down my exposed neck. Fire races through my body. There is something about that spot that drives me wild. Wild with what, I don't know. I exhale and my breathing kicks up its usual notch. Why does he always have to get so damn close to me? Especially when he smells so incredible. His scent is always the same. Apple and spice. Green apple, which I adore the smell of, but he smells so much better. I could just eat him. I close my eyes and regain my composure, his lips still skimming my skin. He's expectant. I can't tell him the full truth. If I don't say it aloud, will it be any less true? So, I opt for silence instead. Maybe he won't bite this time.

After a moment, he pulls back and looks at me. His eyes have turned to that cloudy black again, and I stiffen. He smiles sweetly letting out a small friendly laugh. I smile back and relax. Then he lunges at my neck. He tricked me! Am I actually surprised? Yes, stupid girl. I yelp as his teeth pierce my skin in the same place as before. I wait for the pain, but when it hits me, my head is filled with the image of us in a lover's embrace. My eyes are still open, but all I see is our naked bodies, suspended in mid-air in front of me, woven together by our entwined limbs. Clinging onto the other for our very lives. Our faces buried into one another's neck. It's like we can't get close enough to each other, pressed so hard against one another it's painful. I can feel everything. The chill of Raphael's cold skin against the burning of mine. I watch as I run my hands up and down his back feeling the cool smoothness of his skin against the palms of my hands. It feels beyond real like I'm really touching him. I don't understand where this vivid daydream has come from, but now isn't the time to be having one. I close my eyes tight and try to push the image out of my head, but it won't budge. Like that damn front door that I couldn't shift. No matter how hard I try, it refuses to budge.

Eventually, Raphael licks the wounds and pulls back. The image and sensations disappear the moment his tongue leaves my neck. "Remember, I can do whatever I want to you," he says with a smug look on his face, and then he's gone, locking the door behind him.

I'm left sat there flabbergasted. So, he put that image in my head? But it felt so real. Not just physically but emotionally. It was like there was no one else in the whole entire world but us. I had felt the yearning in his embrace. He wanted me as much as I wanted him but how can that be? The truth is that it isn't that way. He doesn't want me like that. The vision was just a fabricated reality. A fake, a fraud. A sick, twisted dream. I know it could never be like that in real life. Not when he uses such things against me. I honestly don't think he is capable of affection. I think he's too far gone for that. He's let the vampire in him create a great divide between his physical being and his humanity that there may be no saving it. It is probably doomed to sit in limbo between the human world and the vampire world for all eternity and beyond. Too far away for anyone to ever reach it, for me to ever reach it. I question what I have managed to see in him so far; when it's clear there isn't anything good about him. But I know how I feel. I am certain of it. An unknown emotion sneaked up on me, and I didn't realise what it was. It felt so natural and fell into what was normal to me. Now that I know what it is, I'm in so much trouble.

CHAPTER SEVENTEEN

Raphael

I can project images into Rosannah's mind if her reaction is anything to go by. It is most peculiar that I can do that but not brainwash her. When I return to the male, he resembles a bloody pincushion with Evangeline at his throat, Nicholas at his right wrist, and Lawrence at the other. I can't think of anything worse, but it was worth having his blood on me to see Rosannah's reaction. Her fear and anger feeds me in ways she couldn't imagine. But now I want this thing out of my sight before I get too tempted to snap every bone in his body.

"We need to figure to what to do with him," I tell my siblings as they all look up at me. It's a good thing that this guy is still unconscious.

"I vote we kill him." Lawrence grins with red teeth.

"We can't actually kill him even though Lord knows how much I want to," I say with a frown.

"Why not?" asks Nicholas.

"He can't tell us who he works for, vampires no doubt, but he'll eventually lead us to them, and all this about a locator spell is just a load of crap," I tell a frowning Lawrence and Nicholas.

"You suspect he was brainwashed to take Rosannah?" asks Nicholas.

"That's what I'm thinking. In all our years, how much genuine magic have you come across?" I ask him.

"None," he says with a half-smile.

"This is huge, and it's certainly a worry. Obviously, a human who cannot be brainwashed is an enormous liability for vampires. I know The Synod wouldn't do this, so it suggests the information has been leaked or been overheard," I say with a frown.

"So, what's the plan then?" shrugs Evangeline.

"Well, brainwash him with a cover story and send him on his merry way," I say simplistically.

"And not track him?" asks a confused Evangeline.

"He won't be disappearing anytime soon and none one will suspect anything after I've brainwashed him. In the meantime, Lawrence and I will get our supplies that we were so rudely interrupted from getting while Nicholas heals him. I shall then brainwash him once I've returned. Nicholas and Lawrence can drop him off somewhere in the morning," I say.

"What about me?" asks Evangeline.

"You can babysit Rosannah. She is not to know what is going on. It's best that she is kept out of the loop," I say, feeling an immense satisfaction that Rosannah will think the waste of space she calls Alex is dead.

"Fine, but I want a girls' day tomorrow then; you can all disappear for the day." She smiles and races off up the stairs. How on earth do I manage to put up with her? That's right; she's indestructible.

Lawrence and I then run back to the hospital, leaving Nicholas to keep an eye on the male. We get our supplies from Bill, who is more than happy to oblige, no thanks to my brainwashing skills, and head back. When we arrive, we find that Nicholas has healed all of the male's injuries. We have something built into our saliva that heals wounds. It's another means of covering our tracks. We then have a smaller chance of being discovered. It must be nature's way, that's if we're even a part of nature. It takes another four hours after we arrive back for the male to regain consciousness. By this time, we have untied him and sat him in the TV room. He finally starts to come to.

"What the? Oh yeah, I remember now. You caught me trying to rescue your captive and then you beat me up," he says stretching his arms and legs out. That's the understatement of the century. He then looks confused.

"How come I don't feel any pain?" he asks, bewildered. Bringing myself down to his level, I look straight into his eyes.

"That's because you weren't beaten up, you have sustained no injuries here. You came to find someone who is missing, but you found no one. I came home and caught you snooping. After a quick chat, I let you search the house and see that there is no one here but myself. You haven't revealed anything about who you work for and proclaim that you are a private investigator and cannot, for security reasons, give me many details. I offer you a cup of tea in my TV room, which you've just had," I say staring deeply into his eyes.

"Yes," he murmurs.

"You are satisfied and have no reason to return. I then very kindly dropped you off near your home and then you did the usual things you do when you go home after a hard day captive finding. You have never seen any of the vampires or human you have seen here apart from me, Raphael," I tell him.

"I understand," he replies.

"And one more thing." I lean closer to him.

"You ever touch Rosannah again, and I will obliterate you," I say as the image of him on top of Rosannah fills my mind. I grimace and lean back.

"Who's Rosannah?" he asks with confusion.

"No one. Nicholas, Lawrence, get him out of my sight before I break him in two," I say in disgust.

"Sure thing." Nicholas smiles. They pick him up and shoot off. It has taken all night to deal with him, but within minutes, the twins are back.

"Done?" I ask. They both nod.

"Good. We will catch up with our friend in a few days' time." I smile.

CHAPTER EIGHTEEN

Rosannah

The next morning when I wake up, a jubilant Evangeline greets me. "Whoa, has anybody told you that it's illegal to be this happy in the morning?" I say sarcastically as I stretch out under the covers.

"Stop being so silly," she pouts.

"You get to spend some girly time with me. Just you and me, no boys allowed," she squeaks. I scrunch up my face, and she giggles. Once she stops, I look at her seriously. I want to ask her about Alex, but I have a feeling I won't get anything out of her, so I put it on the back burner...for now.

"Okay, okay. Give me ten minutes to get ready," I say as I get out of bed. Shooing her out of my way, I wander almost in a drunken state over to the wardrobe. Randomly grabbing a clean set of clothes, I then lock myself in the bathroom for an ultra-fast and cold wake-up shower. Yelping at the cold water, I try not to jump around while washing myself. I leave the bathroom feeling revitalised and refreshed, only to see that an amused set of twins is now in my room.

"What kind of shower was that?" asks Nicholas.

"Plenty of, err, noise going on," smirks Lawrence.

"Just a very cold one," I retort at him. I hear a little chuckle and see Raphael leaning against the door jam. How did I not notice him there before? I sheepishly look at him as he lightly laughs to himself. The others giggle around me. So, they all think it's funny to laugh at me? They all act like this is normal, like he's normal. Do they have no idea what he is really like? Or do they know and think his behaviour is okay? It's definitely not, but it doesn't disgust me as much as it should. I think that makes me sick on some level or maybe even a sadist. A giddy Evangeline breaks me from my thoughts.

"Don't worry about those two, they're leaving now. So, we can have our girly time!" she says, clapping her hands together. She is definitely Miss Clappy Squeaky today. A feeling of dread settles in my stomach, and I sigh at her over enthusiasm. Raphael snaps his eyes up to mine and watches me as Evangeline ushers the twins past him and out of the room. There's no reaction from him at all. No dark cloudy eyes, no sneering smile. Nothing. How can he stand there as if nothing happened? I begin to ask him about Alex, but he turns and follow the twins. "Let the fun begin!" Evangeline yells as she closes the door behind them.

If I had known what 'girly time' entailed, I would have begged to go with the guys. I mean, I got to try on what Evangeline had ordered. There were bras and thongs. Never worn a thong in my life, and I don't think I'll start now. They look like some kind of torture devices! I'm grateful the guys weren't here. Can you imagine what they would be like when they arrived? I'd never hear the end of it. I've had to resort to layering up vests to keep my bad boys under wraps so that I didn't give the Twins a field day with my nipples pointing aggressively at them. But I know the guys would have saved me from Evangeline. I've lost count of all the makeovers Evangeline gave me. My face is raw and my scalp aches. This girl can do an entire face and hairstyle in less than twenty seconds, and it's as painful as it sounds.

After she had finished abusing my face, we settled down to watch cheesy vampire films. The Lost Boys, Buffy the Vampire Slayer, and Fright Night. Evangeline was crying with laughter, although she cried no actual tears. I found that a little freaky, but her laughter was infectious and I cried the tears for us both! What she found so hysterical was the portrayal of her kind in those movies—garlic does nothing but makes her throw up because she can't digest it; if she couldn't see herself in a mirror, she'd go insane; if someone attempted to stake or behead her, she'd be pretty pissed off, and as for the sun? When the first vampire burst into flames on the screen, she jumped up and screamed at the TV.

She said, and I quote, "Why would the sun do anything to us? It's just heat and light. We just don't like it!" After watching the movies, she flips to a music channel and turns the volume down so we can have a girly chat. She sits next to me, and I jump straight in. Chatting when the films were on was a huge no-no. Well, for me it was.

"Why is Raphael the way he is?" I blurt out. What about poor Alex? I'm sure he's dead, but my priorities have been a little mixed up.

"What on earth do you mean?" Evangeline asks, apparently surprised by my question.

"Surely, you know he torments me?" I ask her. She lets out a little laugh.

"Yes, we are all quite of aware of his treatment of you. We can hear everything." She laughs, pointing to her ears. So, they just let him do it?

"Why do you all let him behave like that?" I ask, slightly annoyed.

"Rosannah, what you need to understand is that we are vampires. We may look harmless but never forget that we drink the very essence of human life. We are predators, and you are our prey. We are not human and many of our human qualities died many years ago. But don't think I or the twins would feed on you; Raphael targeted you," she says, looking incredibly serious. What? I swallow audibly.

"What do you mean targeted?," I ask suspiciously. She suddenly looks like she's said too much.

"Ah, well, not targeted, as such. That's up to Raphael to tell you himself." She smiles at me.

"He won't tell me anything. He treats me so badly, even when he doesn't bite me. You and the twins don't treat me like that. You're all kind to me," I say with a frown.

"Well, Raphael is Raphael. He's different to the rest of us," she says as she gives me an apologetic smile. So, you're all vampires, but Raphael is worse?

"Is he just like that to me or is it how he is to everybody?" I whisper, not wanting to know the answer. Either way isn't good.

"You want to know if he likes you, don't you?" she asks with probing eyes. Ah! Not where I was going! Quick, distract her.

"Where have they gone today?" I say, trying to change the subject. I always seem to be caught out by

Raphael lurking around somewhere, so I best avoid the topic of liking him.

"Oh, I told them we were having a girly day and they had to go out," she says with a smile. They're probably doing something with Alex. Alex!

"What about Alex?" I inquire suddenly.

"Alex?" She looks confused.

"The guy who tried to rescue me," I encourage her.

"Oh, I'm not allowed to talk to you about that," she says, rolling her eyes and shaking her head. So, a direct order from Raphael? What doesn't he want me to know?

"He's killed him, and they're trying to find a place to dump the body. That's what they are doing today!" I yell, jumping up dramatically from the couch. Evangeline slowly shakes her head at me with a pout.

"I can't tell you anything," she sings. I sigh in exasperation.

"That's ridiculous. I can't believe him. He's acting like a jealous child!" I shout in frustration as I begin to pace in front of the TV. "That really isn't a reason to kill someone, not that he should be killing anyone anyway! What's wrong with him?" I say in a rush. Running out of steam, I flop back into my seat.

"He's a vampire," Evangeline says frowning. No shit!

"But surely he wasn't like this when he was human?" I ask, still deflated.

"Rosannah, that was a long time ago. Being immortal and indestructible and having it given to him in one of the worst ways possible has changed him quite dramatically. Not to mention the fact that he's watched people grow old and die when he can't.

You would change, too, if you were put in our shoes," she says with a shrug. Terror grips me.

"I could never be one of you. I'd rather die," I say in a rush of words.

"So, would we have, but we didn't have a choice. You have a choice, but how long it remains a choice, I don't know," she says very carefully.

"What do you mean by that?" I ask.

"I don't mean anything. We just don't know what the future will bring," she says regretfully. I don't believe her at all. She's hiding something, and I'm determined to find out. With Evangeline, it will only be a matter of time before she accidently spills the beans. She suddenly smiles, making me jump. "I know what will help you relax. Come with me," she says and grabs my hands. She pulls me, as gently as a super strong vampire can, to the music room. I strongly doubt that she can make me feel better, but she couldn't make me feel worse, right? "Watch this," she says and winks at me as she sits at the piano. She starts to play long slow notes that sound quite dark and foreboding. Then her fingers are a blur, rushing with ease across the keys. The most pleasing melody plays out, and I can't help a little smile from spreading across my face. She smiles at me as she plays this wonderfully haunting tune. It makes me think of skeletons dancing around in a magnificent ball dressed in silken finery, waltzing with speed. It's crazy!

"What is that?" I ask incredulously.

"It's the 'Death Waltz' by U. N. Owen," she says as she continues to play. Her fingers are everywhere! I'm in utter amazement as she kicks up the speed and her fingers are no longer visible, her eyes still trained on me. The song finishes with her hitting every key at once and then playing a slow teasing melody to fade out. I'm speechless.

"Now, for something a bit slower," she says and starts to play a song I recognise immediately. Soon the lyrics flow from her mouth and her voice is like heaven to my ears. She's playing "Edelweiss," one of my most favourite songs of all time. The song is so beautiful, but she just took it to a whole other level. I stand there riveted, watching her stare into space as she plays and sings the song with more perfection than I ever thought possible. Molding the song with her high notes and making it her own. Kathryn Jenkins has nothing on this girl! Her voice is so powerful. She sounds like her voice is going through an amplifier, but I know it's not. She easily commands volume from the piano so that her voice doesn't drown out the instrument.

I feel tears well up in my eyes. It's the most beautiful thing I've ever heard. A tear escapes the confines of my right eye and slowly trickles down my cheek. Evangeline finishes the song with one high pitch perfect note that warbles wonderfully and fades into silence. She turns and smiles at me. I start to tell her how truly extraordinary that was when something moves in my peripheral vision. I turn to see Raphael standing there looking at me with a soft expression, head tilted slightly to the right. How long has he been there? I wipe the tear from my cheek and make my way to the door. I can't look at him and lower my eyes as I pass him. As lovely as Evangeline's renditions were, I know that poor Alex has greatly suffered at Raphael's hands. He's most likely dead, but I can only assume. The Monstrums locked away his fate, and I'll never know for sure what actually happened to him. I rush to my room and hide away from the monster that is Raphael.

CHAPTER NINETEEN

Raphael

After leaving the house, the twins go off home, and I head over to Rosannah's flat. I have her original key, which I keep along with her bag in my safe located in the study. I let myself in and the smell hits me first. The whole apartment smells of her. Sweet and delicious, the scent is intoxicating. I snoop around her apartment, and I can tell that she's a sensitive person. There are pictures of people all around here. I can't see much resemblance in any of the faces that stare back out at me. If they're all friends, where are her family? A light grey cat pulls me from my thoughts as it darts out from behind the couch and rubs itself against my ankles. I bend down to let it sniff my hand and it starts to purr. It seems to like me, which is unusual. I've never been a pet person, but this cat could grow on me.

The answering machine beeps and I race over to it to see it's full of messages. I press play and very quickly regret it. After hearing a bombardment of messages, I've had enough and push the delete button. That's Rosannah's mother? That woman has serious issues. I pull the plug on the telephone and take a good look at Rosannah's bedroom. I start to look through random drawers and come across her panties. "Ah, there you are," I whisper to them. I snatch a pair up and cover my face with them. Pulling in deep, I let the scent fill my nostrils. Soapy lavender mixed with pheromones. I pull them away with reluctance in my heart, an emptiness in my chest, and a hard on choked by my boxers. Feeling unearthed, I look at the cat, who's just hopped up onto Rosannah's bed. "I won't tell her if you don't," I say putting an index finger to my lips.

"Meow." I put the panties back as I found them and head back into the front room. I spend my time watching TV and just enjoying being in Rosannah's home. As I sit and watch meaningless people talk about meaningless things, the time flies away. Before I know it, it's ten pm. I look down at the cat, which has been using my lap as a bed, and an attempted pincushion.

"Right, kitty, I've got to get back to your mummy. Come on, off you get," I say with a smile and lightly push at the cat, who reluctantly gets off my lap. I connect the phone back in, and it starts ringing immediately. "Yeah, you can keep trying," I smirk at the phone and head back home.

When I get back home, the twins aren't there, but I can hear Evangeline singing her favourite song. I race up to the music room to see her in full-blown song. As wonderful as Evangeline's singing is, Rosannah is who gets my attention. She's so engrossed and emotional by my sister's rendition. Tears trickle slowly down her rosy cheeks. Once Evangeline has done her big finish, I move to get Rosannah's attention. Her eyes snap to mine, and she looks like a rabbit caught in headlights. She hastily wipes a cheek and runs past me. I walk over to Evangeline. "What have you been telling her?" I ask suspiciously.

"Nothing really. She was asking about you." She shrugs.

"What did she ask?" I ask curiously.

"Just why you are the way you are. She also asked about Alex."

"Alex?" I quiz.

"The rescuer. I said I couldn't say anything, and she concluded that you killed him. That's what you wanted, right?" she asks. I let the question hang in the air. Evangeline has a habit of letting things slip. "I may have also told her that you targeted her. I'm off home. Bye." She smiles and races off before I can react. Great. I head downstairs and into the TV room to see that Lawrence is now here.

"When did you scurry in here?" I ask in a foul mood.

"Nicholas and I have been thinking," he starts.

"That must've been a first," I grumble. Lawrence clasps at his chest.

"Ow, brother, ow."

"Get on with it before you succeed in boring me to death," I say lowly. Lawrence straightens himself up.

"We have decided that it's time Rosannah became one of us," he says thoughtfully.

"You won't do any such thing," I growl.

"What does it matter to you if she becomes one of us?" He shrugs.

"It doesn't matter to me," I say trying not to look bothered. Why would I care if she became one of us?

"Well, if it doesn't matter to you, I'll go change her right now then," he says walking off. I race in front of him.

"You will do no such thing," I say, baring my teeth.

"It was only a joke, but oh, my God," he says.

"What?" I say retracting my teeth.

"You do," he says.

"I do what?" I say, getting riled again.

"You actually do," he says with a chuckle.

"Cut it, I'm beginning to get angry," I growl again.

"You love her. You actually love her. I can see it in your eyes. How did I not see it before?" he says getting too close for comfort. I move my face away, but he follows it.

"You have no idea what you're talking about," I say in a rush.

"You didn't deny it, and you didn't even throw your law in my face!" He laughs.

"You are so off the mark. Don't breathe a word of this nonsense to anyone else!" I say pushing him back and walking away. I know I have some kind of feelings for Rosannah but love? He's just playing games with me. Still annoyed, I head upstairs to see Rosannah. I haven't really tormented her today, so I have some making up to do. I do my usual of entering her room in the blink of a human eye. I see no point in locking her door anymore. She's standing by the window looking out. Turning with irritation, she sees it's me.

"Don't any of you ever knock?" she says raising her eyebrows. I smile inwardly and whip over to her.

"Last time I checked, this was my house," I say leaning closer to her and pushing back her hair off her right shoulder. She huffs and walks over to the bed leaving me hanging. This girl really knows how to rattle my cage.

"Unless you're here to tell me about Alex, I don't want to speak to you," she says crossing her arms. I wander over to her like I am stalking prey. Her heart rate kicks up as I reach her.

"You don't need to concern yourself with him any longer," I say playfully, tucking a loose strand of hair behind her left ear. She shivers and bats my hand out of the way.

"You know, if I wanted, I could have stopped you from moving my hand," I say deadpan.

"Yeah, well you just do whatever you want to without any regard for anyone else, don't you?" she asks with slight venom. You certainly don't want to get angry with me because I bite harder. I get my face in hers.

"You know nothing about me," I sneer.

"I know enough." She smiles, unimpressed.

"So, I've been around for three hundred years, and you really know me in what, two days?" I ask incredulously.

"There's too much bad in you. No amount of good is going to override it for me. Alex is a prime example of that. He was trying to rescue me and what did you do to him? You tortured him and then killed him. It makes you incredibly sick," she says with disgust. The anger inside of me boils over, and I lunge for her throat. The warm metallic, salty taste of blood fills my mouth. This time, she actually puts up a struggle, and I can't help but get fully aroused. I clamp onto her with my hands. The more she moves, the tighter I grip. Once she gives up, I lick her wounds and pull back expecting to see fear, but what

I see instead is anger. In one swift motion, well for a human, she slaps me square across the face.

"That's the second time I've let you do that," I say through gritted teeth. She's so angry that tears form in her eyes. She pulls back and aims again. I catch her hand as it swings forward without taking my eyes off hers. Without thinking, I pull her in and kiss her. To my disappointment, she just stands there while I lace my hands up her back, digging my erection into her. I fill her mind with images of her longing to kiss me, but she still doesn't respond. I pull back from her, and she looks horrified.

"When will you understand that I don't want you? Surely the struggle is a big enough sign!" she says, shocked. That hurts a little, but I quickly regain my composure.

"But the struggle makes it so much better," I smirk.

"You're disgusting!" she exclaims.

"News flash, I'm a vampire. I drink blood, I kill fast, and I get so incredibly horny," I say getting closer to her. I place my lips to her ear.

"And I've wanted to screw you since I first saw you," I whisper, spacing out my words with anticipation. She shivers, and I smile to myself. Without looking at her, I turn and leave the room. Lord knows how much I really do want to screw her. Since I first laid my eyes on her, she stirred the wild beast that resides deep inside of me. Something about her screams unobtainable and that just spurs me on even more. Step by step, I will have her. I have had to watch her from a distance like a vulture circling above its next meal, but now I can get up close and it will only be a matter of time before I swoop in for the kill. I know she really wants me. She says she doesn't, but every female I've come across has been attracted to me. There's no way Rosannah can resist, but at the rate I'm going, I'll be the first to buckle. I already have, technically.

CHAPTER TWENTY

Rosannah

And he's gone, again. I stand there dumbfounded. I rub my tingling lips; I can still feel his cold kiss on them. It was my first, and he doesn't even know it. I'm surprised at how much I actually enjoyed it. The feel of his lips on mine and his soft groans had my head in a spin. And his wandering hands, I'm glad it ended there because I might not have been able to stop him had he gone further. I wanted to kiss him back like my life depended on it, but I just froze. And that image he put in my head. It was as vivid as the last! Just like the last time, I was floating around us and could feel everything, again. I have to stay away from him as best I can while being locked in a house that happens to be his home? I'd laugh if it weren't so tragic. I opt for the rather crazy idea of sticking to the twins' sides. I don't think I need to express how desperate I am. I get myself together and rush off to where they are. I halt in the doorway to the TV room. They're sat on the floor caught up in a heated game of Battleship.

"I swear you're cheating! You always cheat!" Nicholas yells at Lawrence.

"No, I'm the cheeky one. You're the cheating one." Lawrence smirks at Nicholas. They are so into their discussion that they don't even notice me standing here. I then spot Raphael, who is sat in a swivel chair facing away from me watching some documentary on the TV. It's a programme on Jupiter and its moons.

How interesting. I never picked him as a space man. I love astronomy, especially anything about Jupiter. It looks like none of them know I'm here. I try to leave, but as I turn to go, a voice stops me in my tracks.

"Ah great, we need an umpire, sit," demands Nicholas without even looking up at me.

"Damn it," I whisper. How did he know?

"I'm a vampire," he smirks. So I can see what they're both doing, I reluctantly sit next to the game, which is laid out between them. Raphael turns in his chair to face us, giving me a suspicious look. Is it suspicious if I actively choose to spend time with the twins? I guess it is. I risk a glance at Raphael, who gives me a simmering dark grey look back and 'I get so incredibly horny' pops unwelcomely into my head. I blush and he smirks causing me to blush even more. I look down at the boards as the Twins continue playing, oblivious to what else is happening. Thank goodness. I refuse to look at Raphael again as he continues to stare at me through fifty-seven more games of Battleship. I could feel his gaze boring into me like a drill, daring me to look at him. Even with the twins here, he can still find a way to toy with me. I focus on the twins' hands as they moved like blurs. It is incredibly hard to keep a track of what they are doing, but it's clear that Lawrence is not only cheeky but also a cheat. I could just about gather that he moved some of his ships, but in the blink of an eye, I can miss many moves. "Do you want to play a game?" asks Nicholas.

"Sure, but you'll have to move a lot slower." I laugh.

"Of course," says Lawrence with a grin, giving Nicholas a cheeky look. Nicholas returns his grin. "Right, we can play Ludo. What colour do you want to be," Lawrence asks me.

"Yellow, please," I say with a smile.

"Why yellow?" he asks puzzled.

"So I can be the ray of sunshine on the board," I say as I smile even more.

"You already are a ray of sunshine," Nicholas mutters, his expression changing to one I don't recognise. How bizarre. Lawrence pulls me from my thoughts.

"You still staring, Raph? No matter how hard you stare at her, her clothes won't fall off." He laughs. Raphael gets up and walks off in a huff. I knew there had to be a good reason to hang out with these two. They are a menace and a bit much sometimes, but right now they are helping tremendously. The taunts the twins throw at Raphael act like a repellent. As much as I love to be near him, I think it best that I keep a barrier between us. A barrier comprised of a set of very naughty vampire twins. We laugh and joke for hours playing Ludo. They find the speed I play at quite amusing, and surprise, surprise, I don't win a single game. When they go to leave, I insist they stay. I don't want them to leave me alone with Raphael. My insistence warrants some 'she's a stalker' looks from them.

"Very weird, Nicholas."

"Very weird, Lawrence." They throw at each other. I just pretend that I love their company which causes more looks, especially from Evangeline when she heads home, but the twins were pretty chuffed about it. It rubbed their egos up the right way, but if they had even the slightest inclination to the truth, they would feed me to Raphael like a zebra to a lion. It turns out they're staying anyway but had me pleading just for entertainment—vampire swines!

I manage to stick with them for three solid days, pissing off Raphael and making Evangeline pout more times than Posh Spice on a photo shoot. I really get to know the twins in that time and discover that they are much more alike than I had realised. They are both just as cheeky as the other is, and both terrible liars and cheats. I also learn that most people can never tell them apart with the exception of Raphael and Evangeline. Even their own parents couldn't and I'm quite chuffed that I can differentiate them. They are identical, but I just know which one is which. On the fourth night, I can't persuade them to stay again. No amount of puppy dog eyes is going to win them over this time. I head to my room and decide it's probably best if I get to sleep as Raphael might not bug me then. I get as far as washing and changing. I pull back the blankets on the bed when Raphael bursts in. I go to scramble back to the other side of the room but only make it a few feet. In a flash, he's in front of me with his teeth on display. "Don't," I whimper, cowering away from him, knowing he wants to bite me, again.

"Using my brothers to get away from me?" he whispers and tuts. He pulls my head to the side and sinks his teeth into my tender neck. I scream at him to stop, but he groans and begins to suck. God, he's enjoying this; he always enjoys this. A fire rushes through me, and I suddenly imagine him clamping down between my legs. Him and his damn visions! It feels just as real as the last two except this time I have a first person view. In this one I'm laying down, watching him lick and suck while I'm moaning and writhing. I know this is all in my head, but it feels so real. I push away from him to see he's grinning with my blood around his mouth. He wipes it off on his sleeve, staring at me intensely with jet black eyes. I'm so angry with him.

"Stop putting things like that in my head," I spit. He backs me up against the wall, pinning me with his hands on my shoulders.

"I'm only showing you what you want to see," he whispers in my ear. I struggle out from his hands, but he just grips me tighter.

"Ow, it's not what I want to see," I say. I'm sure it's not.

"Of course, it is," he says with his dark eyes on mine. He licks his lips. "I'll have you screaming in the next one. You look like a screamer to me." He grins as he looks me up and down. This has to end, now. I can't take this much longer.

"I wouldn't know," I say reluctantly.

"What do you mean? Of course, you know if you're a screamer. When you've had sex, you either screamed or not." He laughs softly. I look at the floor.

"I wouldn't know because I've never..." I wait, but there's no response. I look up at him, and his brow is furrowed. "You know," I hint. He looks confused and releases me. Do I have to spell it out? Bloody hell. "I'm a virgin," I say with conviction. The confusion drops from his face.

"Oh...my...God," he says with slow horror. He backs away from me like I'm the most frightening thing in the world and suddenly disappears, slamming the door shut behind him. What the hell? I go and sit on the bed, my mind blank. I sit confused for a while, my head trying to wrap itself around what just happened. Finally, my brain kicks back into gear. If that's all it took to put him off, I should have told him in the beginning. Then another thought dawns on me. Why did he react like that? Does he think it's disgusting that I'm a virgin? There's nothing wrong with being a virgin! I start to fill with anger and leap from the bed. I want to know what Raphael's problem is. Whether it's the virgin part or the fact that I'm one doesn't matter, I just want to know what freaked him out. I'm going to go and find him.

CHAPTER TWENTY-ONE

Raphael

I can't get away from her quick enough. All this time I've been playing with her and I had no idea. It all makes sense now. That's why she froze when I kissed her! I was probably her first! It was just a game before, but a game I have indeed lost. No, no, this has gone terribly wrong. My one weakness, why did she have to be my one weakness?! I head into the kitchen and pace.

"Whoa there, brother, that's one heck of a face you've got on there," says Nicholas as he watches me go back and forth. "This isn't Wimbledon," he jokes.

"How could I not know? How could I have been so blind?" I ask incredulously.

"Okay, calm, deep, vampire breaths," Nicholas says soothingly. I turn and glare him.

"Are you a complete idiot?" I spit at him. His face scrunches up in confusion. "Are you trying to tell me that you did not just hear what happened?" I ask. Then Lawrence and Evangeline walk into the room.

"What's going on?" Evangeline quizzes.

"I'm trying to figure out what's got him all worked up." Nicholas shrugs.

"Oh, I've got this. Is it three words?" chuckles Lawrence. I grab him by the throat and lift him off the floor as I talk to the others.

"None of you have a clue of what's going on?" I ask ignoring Lawrence's struggles.

"Raph, we have no idea what you're going on about. We don't always listen in on you," says Evangeline. I let go of Lawrence, who straightens himself up.

"Yeah, most of the time you're boring, and we're so over you biting Rosannah," he says as he smoothes his shirt down.

"I've been enjoying toying with her, teasing her, tormenting her! I had it all planned out. See how far I could push her. Wind her up ever so slightly each time so I could watch the grand finale! Now, that's all ruined! She has the one thing I didn't even think of and now I'm mad with burning desire to take it from her! It's insatiable! For her own good, it's best I don't go anywhere near her!" I say as I continue to pace.

"It's finally happened. He's gone mad," Lawrence states, feigning concern. I turn and look at him.

"This is no joking matter," I growl.

"What could she possibly have that has driven you to this state?" asks Nicholas.

"She's a virgin," I say deadpan, and with that, the twins burst out laughing. "It is so beyond funny, it's untrue," I say, gritting my teeth.

"Oh, but it is," says Lawrence, who's now in stitches.

"Raph, I don't understand the problem, or why it's so funny for that matter," says a confused Evangeline. This just makes the twins laugh even more.

"You see, it's like this," says Lawrence putting an arm around Evangeline's neck to support his weight while he's still laughing.

"Don't," I warn.

"Oh, but I can't help myself, dear brother." He grins at me. "Raph always plays the big bad and nothing drives him crazy like a virgin. Like a cloak of darkness that swallows the day, he creeps in like an agile fog. Stealing innocence away and ravishing fear like it was a fine and delicate wine. Once it's all over, he makes them forget he was ever there. The true vampire whore that he is. But...I can't, I can't. Nicholas, you finish," says Lawrence, who collapses on the floor in fits of laughter. Nicholas takes Lawrence's place around Evangeline's neck.

"But this time, he doesn't want to take that innocence away, and even if he did, unfortunately for him, he can't make her forget. So, even though his pants might be driving, she's telling them where to go. Every time he sees her, she'll be wearing her virginity like a white surrender flag. A ripe and juicy apple there for the plucking but not to eat. Such conflict. And so, the tormented is now the tormentor! You'll have Raph trying to hide from Rosannah as it will be torture just to look upon her, but ironically, she's a prisoner in his house. A prisoner he has no choice but to keep. Every time he sees her, it's going to be hilarious!" Nicholas says and collapses, too.

"This is meant to be funny? I don't get it," says a bewildered Evangeline. "Just get over yourself and seduce her," she says shrugging her shoulders.

"He can't. That's what's so funny," laughs Lawrence from the floor.

"Why not?" puzzles Evangeline. Lawrence jumps up.

"Shall I tell her or should you?" He grins.

"I swear if you so much as mutter another word I'll..."

"Because he's in love with her," Lawrence smirks, cutting me off.

"Damn you," I growl.

"Oh my goodness. Of course. You are totally in love with her. Why didn't I see it before? I can see it radiating from you." Evangeline smiles.

"He won't even deny it!" says Lawrence. I stand there speechless for a second. It's just enough time for him to disappear.

"He is beyond lucky that he just left," I say finding my voice.

"Don't worry, Raph. I'll have a chat with Rosannah and sort this all out," chirps Evangeline, who also disappears before I can do anything. Great.

CHAPTER TWENTY-TWO

Rosannah

I march my way to the door and open it. Raphael didn't lock the door in his panic. Grrrr, that just winds me up even more. Continuing my search for him, I come across Lawrence instead at the bottom of the stairs, and he has a half smirk on his face. Great. It's as if he's been waiting for me. "I thought you left," I say, slightly irritated.

"That's what we told you, but it doesn't mean we did," he says as the smirk grows larger. I can't believe him! Actually, is it any surprise?

"Where's Raphael?" I demand, ignoring his expression.

"He's hiding from you. It seems the only thing in this entire world that can scare an indestructible immortal like Raph is little old you and your V plates." He giggles.

"This really isn't funny and my V Plates are none of your damn business. I honestly don't know what his problem is..." Lawrence cuts me off.

"It's hilarious! He has this thing about virgins. He was controlled before, but now that he's found out you're one, he's a beast for you. It torments him having you here and seeing him suffer is the most entertaining thing ever," he says trying to keep a serious face.

I suddenly feel quite frightened and shocked. He had control before? I can't even imagine what he'd be like now. My heart races and my head spins at the thought. I would love nothing more than to see him lose control, but I can't let that happen. What a story that would make for mum, though. That would just shut her right up, for once, but Raphael and I can't have any kind of relationship. It just wouldn't work. Although it will be almost unbearable, I'm glad that Raphael will keep away from me. But how are we going to do that when we are in the same house?

"Oh, your face makes it even funnier!" Lawrence says bursting out laughing, pulling me back from my thoughts. "Now I know why you were hanging around with Nicholas and me. We thought you might have had a little crush on us but figured out that you just wanted to hide from the big bad wolf. If we had known the truth, we would have delivered you to his bedroom door," he says giggling. Wow, so they are condoning that Raphael should practically rape me?

"Don't even try to act like you wouldn't love Raphael to have his wicked way with you. We all know you'd absolutely love it," he says, suddenly serious. Ah, so they think I'd be a willing participant. Well, that would stop it from being rape, but surely the fact that I hung out with them would be a clear sign that I don't want anything to happen. Maybe not. My thoughts turn to food. I try my luck.

"Well, would you be so kind as to get me something to eat from the kitchen? I don't want to risk coming across him," I ask as sweetly as I can.

"No way. I'm not making this any easier for you. I've got my wager on Raphael winning this." He laughs while I scowl at him. Of course, he wouldn't help!

"You're a complete fiend, you know that!" I scathe and walk back up the stairs to my room.

"Err, hello. I'm a vampire," he yells after me, still laughing as I slam the bedroom door. From then on, I only risk sneaking out when I absolutely have to. No one locks the door anymore. Raphael doesn't visit me, Evangeline forgets, and I bet the twins leave it deliberately unlocked. They think this whole thing is hilarious. Lawrence believes that Raphael will win, and Nicholas thinks I will. When I sneak out, they call him, just to see me in a flurry of panic, rushing to my room like a scared little mouse. Sometimes they don't even see me. They can hear me, and sometimes I don't even get past opening the door. Raphael never appears when they call him, but that's not the point! The twins are also always making new bets about the outcome. I have no idea what they win, but they're always making bets. Gambling vampires. I suppose if you've been around for as long as they have, you have to do something to pass the time.

With my prison extended to the whole house and grounds, I have free run of it but my newfound freedom isn't that liberating. I'm still sneaking around, but I don't know why I bother when they can all still hear me. It's the morning, and my belly is rumbling. I risk a quick visit to the kitchen like I've done before. So far, Raphael and I have avoided each other. Not being able to see him has almost driven me insane. It's a small taste of what life would be like without him, and it's a barren, desolate world that stabs away at me with a blunt knife.

I was afraid of this that I would fall for him in a big way and get hurt. And that is exactly what's happened. As I reach the bottom of the stairs, I'm glad I haven't bumped into the terrible twosome. This could be one of the occasions they let me get a plate of food before calling Raphael. A pained voice coming from the TV room stops me. The door's shut, which is very unusual. Well, for this place anyway.

"I can't stand it. Honestly, I can't." It's Raphael and although I shouldn't, I listen some more. "It's eating away at me. I'm keeping away, but I can still hear everything, smell everything. I can't wait much longer. I have to..." I stop listening; I don't want to hear any more. That teaches me for eavesdropping. Spooked, I race to the kitchen and hear the twins giggle from somewhere in the house. I can't see them but hearing them is enough. Little monsters knew I was there listening! I'm just about to bolt back upstairs when Evangeline speaks up from in the kitchen. I didn't even notice she was in there. She's sat at the breakfast bar reading a newspaper. If she's here and the twins are lurking, who the hell was Raphael talking to?

"Oh, hi Rosannah, was just going to pop up after reading this." She smiles, lowering her paper. "It seems that you're the talk of the house," she says with a knowing smile. She knows? Of course, she does.

"Oh, not you, too." I sigh, my shoulders sagging as I walk over to her. I'm safe when I'm with her. Raphael wouldn't do anything when I'm with any of them. Would he? I mentally push the thought away. She lifts the paper slightly back up and appears to be reading again.

"Why don't you just make it easier on yourself and give him what he wants," she states like it's nothing.

"What?" I ask, my heart suddenly racing.

"My brother, the one who wants in your pants. Why don't you just give him what he wants? We'll all go out and leave you both to it," she says bluntly. Oh, my God, did she really just say that?

"I can't just, you know." I can't hide my shock. She closes her paper and looks at me with a small huff.

"Why not?" she asks, shrugging her shoulders so fast it's a blur.

"Because I'm a virgin," I whisper. The words so quiet, they barely leave my lips. I know the twins are within vampire earshot.

"So? That's egged him on even more. You really shouldn't have told him that," she says raising an eyebrow at me.

"I thought it would make him understand why I didn't respond to his advances the way he would have liked. And I kind of hoped it would put him off," I say with a frown. My plan clearly hadn't worked.

"I say you give it to him, virgin or not." She smiles. The fact that none of this bothers her bothers me even more.

"Because I'm saving myself for someone I love. I'm not just going to..." The weight of embarrassment pushes down on my shoulders, and I feel my cheeks burn. "...let your brother steal my virtue," I say in a rush. I know that I love him, but I really can't go there.

"Well, at least you've told him now." She smiles, looking over my right shoulder. Horror settles over me as I turn to the door and see Raphael leaning up against the frame with his arms crossed. He looks so beautiful, and it's so good to see him, but my happiness at seeing him quickly dissolves. He looks like he wants to devour me with those cloudy black eyes I've seen way too much of. He looks so incredibly hot and my pulse kicks up another notch. My cheeks flush even more. Why am I standing here ogling him? We're trying to hide from one another. I run past him and past a laughing Lawrence and Nicholas. I get back to my room, and I can still hear them laughing, so I flop onto my bed and shove a pillow over my head to drown out the sound. I'm happy to sacrifice some oxygen if it means I don't have to listen to them cackling away.

CHAPTER TWENTY-THREE

Raphael

"How you holding up, bro?" asks Lawrence sincerely.

"I can't stand it. Honestly, I can't." I sigh. "It's eating away at me. I'm keeping away, but I can still hear everything, smell everything. I can't wait much longer; I have to...do something," I exclaim in frustration. The twins laugh.

"Damn the pair of you," I say and leave them falling about in the TV room. As I enter the hallway, I can see Rosannah standing in the kitchen. Those two knew she was there. They distracted me! I turn to look at them, and they just whistle as if they know nothing. Rosannah's voice pulls my attention back to her.

"Oh, not you, too." She sighs as she disappears further into the kitchen. It's torture being near her, but I have to know what they're saying, so I walk to the kitchen. Leaning against the doorframe, I cross my arms and listen. Evangeline's eyes quickly flash to mine and back to Rosannah, so quickly she wouldn't see it.

"Why don't you just make it easier on yourself and just give him what he wants," states Evangeline.

"What?" asks Rosannah with shock, her heart drumming in her chest. The twins appear behind me. I turn and hold up my finger, signaling to them to be quiet.

"My brother, the one who wants in your pants. Why don't you just give him what he wants? We'll all go out and leave you both to it," says Evangeline. Very tactful, Evangeline. Very tactful.

"I can't just, you know," says Rosannah. I can smell her sweat as it moistens her delicate skin. My mouth starts to salivate.

Why not?" Evangeline asks.

"Because I'm a virgin," she whispers. I hear a quiet snigger from the twins. I glare at them, and they stop. I then turn back to the kitchen.

"So? That's egged him on even more. You really shouldn't have told him that." Yes, I agree. You really shouldn't have told me that.

"I thought it would make him understand why I didn't respond to his advances the way he would have liked. And I kind of hoped it would put him off." You reacted exactly the way I wanted. Petrified.

"I say you give it to him, virgin or not." I second that.

"Because I'm saving myself for someone I love. I'm not just going to..." Someone she loves? "...let your brother steal my virtue." Oh, I could do more than just steal her virtue!

"Well, at least you've told him now." Evangeline smiles, looking over at me. Rosannah turns very slowly to look me straight in the eyes. The horror on her face overshadows her magnificent beauty. She looks petrified, but it softens and I feel immensely delighted. The elation of it turns me on, and I can feel the constriction of my jeans from my erection. I see joy dance behind her eyes and crimson engulf her cheeks. It takes all I have not to chase after her as she flies past me. I would love nothing more than to have my wicked way with her. The twins enter the kitchen laughing, pulling me from my thoughts. Erection deflated. "See, I told you that I'd get to the bottom of it." Evangeline smiles.

"Yes, she doesn't love me." I try to smile. The pang in my redundant heart is almost like a physical blow.

"So, The Synod wants the next big meeting here," Nicholas says.

"I knew it wouldn't be long before they wanted to get their noses officially stuck back into my business. To look at her is the most they can do," I say. The twins growl lightly. "Wow, you care about what actually happens to Rosannah?" I ask.

"We care about anyone who has captured your heart." Evangeline smiles.

"I..."

"Yeah, yeah, we know. You don't love her. Well, we're all heading home to give you two some time." She grins. I suddenly panic.

"Why? Why would you do that?" I say, worried. Nicholas walks off, but Lawrence comes over to me and puts his hands on my shoulders.

"Raphael, Lords knows how much you two just need to fuck. Just go and get it over with done with. Do us all a favour and put yourself out of your misery because you are one annoying douche at the moment," he says seriously.

"Where's Nicholas gone?" I wonder aloud.

"Oh, he's just worried he's going to lose our bet. I bet you'll get your way and he's betting that Rosannah won't give it up." He smiles.

"Evangeline...can you take Rosannah shopping for the next Synod..."

"I know. Don't worry, I've got it covered," interrupts Evangeline. I smile at her. I know I can definitely rely on her when it involves shopping. Rosannah is beautiful the way she is, but I know Evangeline will work her magic. I want to rub The Synod's nose in it at the next meeting. I watch as Lawrence and Evangeline leave and hesitantly close the door behind them. I know they've left me alone with her, but I'm still going to try my best to stay away. I go and get ready for bed. Laying down, I can hear Rosannah's breathing, and I smile to myself. Then, I start to hear something else that has me sitting up in my bed.

CHAPTER TWENTY-FOUR

Rosannah

After a while, the laughter stops and I feel a rush of relief. Bumping into Raphael was inevitable and I was a complete idiot even to think I wouldn't. I get up and head to the bathroom for a nice shower. As I undress, my thoughts turn to Raphael and that encounter. He looked so calm and collected while I was falling apart inside. Maybe Lawrence was lying; maybe he was just playing one of his annoying games. But then again, Raphael bolted as soon as I told him that I was a virgin. Maybe Lawrence, for once, was telling the truth! Still, seeing him was bittersweet. Exhilarating, yet abhorrent at the same time. Will I ever be able to admire just his beauty without seeing the beast? I think back to when I first met him. He was nothing more than a magnificent superficial. A sexually charged effigy to masturbate over. Not that I've ever done that. Never felt the need to but Brianna was always going on about her rabbit. She first told me about it when she offered to buy me one for Christmas. She was singing its praises, and I was flabbergasted. I told her that Marmalade would eat it. Once she fully explained what it was, I laughed my head off! Suffice to say, I did not find one under my tree come Christmas morning.

Laughing to myself, I turn the shower on. As the water washes over me, my thoughts turn again to

Raphael. Why am I even scared of what he might do? Apart from biting me, he can't really do anything with the others around here. And at least one of them is always here. Especially one of the terrible twosome, who love to make the situation worse. Or in their words 'more sporting.'

My thoughts then turn the visions. Those unbelievably vivid visions. Is that what Raphael would do to me if given the chance? Again, inner turmoil fills me. On the one hand, I'm screaming inside for the beautiful, enchanting male to take me, but on the other hand, I don't want the egotistical psychotic monster. Again, he can torture me without even doing anything!

I take to scrubbing myself hard to distract myself. Once showered, I get dressed and climb into bed. Closing my eyes, I try to fall into the land of nod, but instead of peaceful slumber, all I can think about is him. I try to block him from my mind, but I can't. Raphael's visions pour through the floodgates and surge my mind. The kissing, the groping, the sucking, they all savage my rumination.

I start to feel myself moisten. I writhe in the confines of my bed as I begin to ache and throb. I squeeze my legs together as little groans escape my lips. I take a deep breath in. "Oh, my God," I murmur as I try to suppress the temptation to touch myself. The door flings open and then shuts. I stop immediately. Oh no, I've been heard. Of course, he heard me! I throw the covers off and sit straight up. Raphael is standing in front of the door. I can see behind his pure black eyes that he's unhinged. The barrier has broken down, and he's free. Dressed in only his boxer briefs, they reveal just how aroused he is. Oh shit. I know why he's here, and it's not going to happen. I get up on my knees. "Leave, now," I order him. He's at me in split seconds, his mouth colliding painfully with mine. His lips are soft and cool, his kiss hungry with need. His hands are gripping my waist, and I can't help but kiss him back just as eager. Small moans escape my throat but are swallowed by his mouth. His hands travel down my back and under my vest. This is going too far. Warring with myself, I pull back from him and grab his hands. "No, Raphael," I say, trying to catch my breath.

"Yes. I have to fuck you, and I have to fuck you now. I can't hold on anymore," he says through gritted teeth. Oh, my God!

"No," I squeak in protest. No? You mean yes! No, you mean no! He pulls his hands from mine and grabs at my vest. I feel the cotton chafe and burn against my skin as it gives way. Exposed, I hide my breasts with my hands. He leans forward and looks at my covered chest, his top lip curling into a light growl. He puts his arms behind my legs and in one swift movement pulls them up in front of me, causing me to lay on my back. With him now kneeling between my legs, I shake my head slowly, no longer able to voice my objections.

"Yes," he whispers as he lowers over me and plants another kiss on my lips. As I kiss him back, he finds my tongue and softly starts to lick it. My muscles clench, and I groan into his mouth. Damn it! He growls and reaches down for my panties. In one final attempt to resist him, I grab his wrists. But in the blink of an eye, he pins my hands above my head. Pulling back from his kiss, something flashes behind his eyes, but it's gone as quick as it came. He leans over to my right ear. "Give in to me," he whispers. Breathing heavily, I surrender and close my eyes. I won't fight it anymore.

He lets go of my hands and moves my left arm out of the way as he sinks his teeth into my neck. I cry out. Pleasure spliced perfectly with pain. As fire races through my body, he begins to suck at the wounds, caressing them with his mouth. I moan with delight as he seals them off with his tongue. He kneels up and pulls my legs up in front of me. Sliding his hands down my thighs, he quickly pulls my panties off, throwing them on the floor. My legs shamefully fall back down and apart revealing myself to him. He hovers over me and plants a quick kiss on my lips before going to my breasts and taking my left nipple in his mouth. He gently nips and sucks the tender nib. The sensations shoot deep down, making me cry out.

"Ah," Raphael growls and traces his right hand down my body to my throbbing core. He slides his fingers between the lips and pulls back from my nipple with a hiss.

"You're so wet," he says in amazement. What did you expect? The Sahara Desert? He looks into my eyes, and I think I can see something else there, but then it's gone again in a flash. Lowering to kiss me again, he licks my lips and tongues my mouth. He slowly inserts one finger into me. I wince into his mouth at the sharp burning pain of being stretched. He pulls back. "You're so tense," he whispers. No shit, Sherlock. He carries on kissing me while he begins to slide in and out of me. The pain begins to fade, and the pleasure is sensational, radiating out from our physical connection. Confidence builds up, and I meet his thrusts. He then inserts another.

Again, it hurts and I wince, but after a few minutes, the pain disappears and the pleasure returns. He pulls back from our kiss to look at me, putting the arm he's leaning on behind my shoulders to cradle me. He presses up inside of me and a new tingling starts and spread. I moan as my muscles tighten up. I don't know what's happening, but it feels so damn good. He looks down at his fingers and then back at me.

"You're going to come," he says, pleasure wrapping his words, desire weighting his eyelids. I look into his eyes and can see what was there before. I can't tell what it is and confusion crosses my face. Then I feel a detonation of sensation and cry out, throwing my head back. "Yes," Raphael hisses as he quickens his pace. My muscles tense and I convulse as waves of pleasure power through me. Squeezing my thighs around his hand, I rock on his fingers. Raphael keeps going until the waves fade. I lift my head to look at him.

"What was that?" I ask breathlessly.

"That was your first orgasm," he says, taking his fingers out of me. Oh, so that's what one is? Damn, I never knew they could feel like that. No wonder Brianna loves her rabbit! But a rabbit is no comparison to Raphael. He holds his fingers up so I can see the glistening wet on them. He puts his soaked fingers in his mouth and sucks it off of them. Closing his eyes, he savours the flavour and moans. Wow, that's actually a turn on. He pulls his hand out from behind my shoulder and leans down to kiss me, teasing my tongue with his until I whimper.

He pulls back and looks at my lips. "I've got to taste more of you," he says tracing them with his thumb. Starting at my neck, he kisses his way down to my breasts, stomach, and down an inner thigh. I twitch as he nips his way back up the other inner thigh. He kisses my sex, and I yelp. With a small laugh, he parts the opening with his tongue and clamps down, sucking and licking the hypersensitive nub just as he did to my tongue. His cool tongue tickles, and I look down to watch him. I feel the pleasure starting to build, and I know what's coming. I can't do that in his mouth! I start to whimper and moan rocking on my hips.

"I can't," I just about manage to say. Propping myself up on my elbows, I clamber back pulling away from him. He growls and reaches forward, wrapping his arms under my thighs and pulls me back with a tug.

"No, you don't," he warns. He clamps back down with his mouth again and holds me in place with two flat palms spayed across my stomach. Within seconds, my muscles tighten.

"Oh, God...Ah." I come spectacularly in his mouth. He rides the waves of passion out by thrusting his tongue in and out of me. Pleasure spiked with pain as his tongue stretches me out further. Once the convulsions have stopped, he stands up. I go on my elbows and move up the bed to ogle his body. He's very muscular and sculpted. He looks hard like carved marble and looks as smooth and as light as white silk. His washboard abs ripple down into a much defined V shape. I clock his erection in his tight boxer briefs. It's working its way around his right thigh.

He catches me eyeing up his manhood and raises an eyebrow. Taking off his boxers, his erection springs up and hits his belly. It's huge and bulging. It's wider than my wrist and longer than my hand. I don't care what Brianna has said about the bigger, the better. There's no way that will fit! He pulls me back down the bed so I'm flat on my back. He hitches my knees up and pulls them apart. I look up at him with panic as he places his hips between mine, the end of his erection pressing against my entrance.

"Don't worry, it'll only hurt a little bit," he soothes. He kisses me and wraps his arms beneath me, working his hands down my back. I can feel all of his weight on my chest. He's pretty damn heavy, and it crushes some of the air from my lungs. He grabs my ass tightly and lunges forward. The pain is sharp and burns like before, but this is much more intense. I yell out in pain, but his mouth stifles it. He pulls back from our kiss, leaning up on his elbows to look at me. I draw in a deep breath, glad to be free of his weight. His brow then furrows.

"I'm going to go slow," he whispers as he starts to slide in and out of me. It's so tight and still hurts. I whimper in pain for some time until it subsides. Only then does it start to feel really good. I breathe heavily, trying not to moan aloud. Moving in time with him, I start to sweat. Looking down between our bodies, I watch him sliding in and out of me. It's the most erotic thing I've ever seen. Rolling my eyes, I throw my head back growling. Eventually, I look back at Raphael.

That look is back again. I still don't fully understand it, but I feel like I can look right through him. Like I can look beneath his mask and see what's underneath. He's absolutely beautiful, and I have to hold back a sob. Feeling emotional, I need to have him closer and so I wrap my arms and legs tight around him causing him to collapse on top of me with a loud groan. His weight is crushing, but I'm beyond caring. His thrusts deepen and his face is just millimetres from mine. I start to moan with him as he hits a new spot deep within me. I soon feel another climax build up again. My moans start to get higher and more frantic as he drives me closer.

"Oh, God," I moan.

"That's it," he says, his voice laced with desire.

"Ahhh," I scream out as all my muscles tighten and pleasure blasts through me again. Raphael moans loudly, too, and tenses up. I feel him convulse with me. Once the waves have stopped, my legs and arms drop from around him and he kisses me hard, cupping my face in his hands. He then starts to thrust again. This happens most of the night until he pulls out and rolls to the side, pulling me with him so that I lay partially on his chest. I'm so worn out that I fall into a deep sleep.

CHAPTER TWENTY-FIVE

Raphael

I lay there for hours watching in awe as Rosannah sleeps. I've never experienced anything like it. I mean, I been with many women. Both vampire and human. I have plenty of experience there but not so much on the emotional side of things. As the sun rises, I reluctantly leave her and return to my room to take a shower and get dressed. I know the others left so this could happen, but I don't want them knowing. I can't explain why I just want to keep it between Rosannah and me. The others will never know unless one of us tells them. I head downstairs, and a grinning Lawrence greets me. I can't help but smile.

"Is that the smile of a vampire who just got laid?" he asks, raising his eyebrows. I growl at him. "Whoa there, big boy, it's not my fault you can't get your leg over." He laughs, palms up as if something invisible is too hot to touch.

"I'm going to go see Rosannah." Evangeline smiles. What the hell? I have to stop her. I can't have her seeing those sheets!

"Why don't you plan out your shopping trip first?" I suggest, hoping it will distract her. My plan works.

"You're right!" she exclaims, running off.

"I'm going to watch the box." Nicholas shrugs while Lawrence heads off to the kitchen. Now's the right opportunity. I rush up the stairs and stand outside Rosannah's door. I can hear that she's in the shower. In a flash, I put on new sheets, wrapping up the old ones and shoot into my bedroom just as Rosannah emerges from the bathroom. I'm too fast for her to see me. I go into my closet and put the sheets in the laundry basket. I sit and wait in my room until I hear her eventually go downstairs. If the others see us together, it will rouse suspicion. I'm meant to be avoiding being alone with her. Knowing the coast is clear, I head downstairs to the kitchen where Lawrence and Rosannah are. When I enter the room, I clap eyes with her and watch as she physically stiffens in front of me. What the hell is wrong with her?

"Ah, this has to be good," Lawrence starts to joke.

"Rosannah looks like she's seen a ghost, oh, wait a minute." He laughs. I watch the horror play out on Rosannah's face. That actually hurts.

"Shut up, Lawrence," I snap at him. Lawrence just carries on laughing. I think I made the right decision in not letting the others know that I've had sex with Rosannah. I whiz to the fridge, get a glass of blood, and sit down at the breakfast bar. I was hoping I could drink in peace but with Rosannah and Lawrence here, it's nearly impossible. Once she's finished her breakfast, she rushes to the sink in a hurry to leave the kitchen, to get away from me. I don't understand. Lawrence rushes to do her washing up. As he's so eager, I race over and give him my glass. He quietly growls at me, and my lips twitch a smile back at him. While he's busy washing up at human speed, I risk a glance at Rosannah, who's staring at my dick. When she looks up at me, I raise an eyebrow at her.

"So when are we sorting out this meeting?" asks Lawrence, distracting me. Rosannah seizes the opportunity to run off. Damn it.

"Hold on." I pull out my phone and text Mathias. When is next meeting? R. Within seconds, my phone beeps. "Tomorrow evening at yours, 7 pm. All partners, too. M," I read out.

"That's not much notice," Lawrence says as he raises his eyebrows.

"That doesn't bother me. It's the partners who have me slightly suspicious. They must really want to show Rosannah off." I frown.

"Well, we'll all keep an eye on her," Lawrence ensures.

"Where are the others?"

"I'm here," pipes up Evangeline as she appears in the room. "Nicholas is getting himself a suit. He heard you read out the text. You know he has literally hundreds, but he needs a new one." She shrugs.

"Evangeline, you can take Rosannah shopping whenever you like," I tell her.

"Well, she's enjoying the sun in the garden at the moment. I'll take her tomorrow." She smiles. In the garden? I leave them there and head upstairs to watch Rosannah out of my bedroom windows.

"Dude, staring at her won't get you anywhere," says Lawrence, who's popped into my room unannounced and uninvited.

"I'm not staring at her. I simply like the view," I say, my eyes fixed on her.

"If you don't love her, I'm human," Lawrence says as he leaves.

CHAPTER TWENTY-SIX

Rosannah

As I stir awake, I realise that I'm no longer wrapped in Raphael's arms. I slowly open my eyes and see he isn't here. Was it all a dream? Confused, I get out of bed and see blood on the sheet. The stark reality hits me as I stare at the evidence of my lost virginity. My panties and the remnants of my vest are on the floor. Feeling abandoned and empty, I stifle a painful gasp. I know that I love him, but I feel dirty and used. All I want right now is to wash it all away as quickly as possible. I rush into the bathroom and turn the shower on. Letting the temperature build up, I get in and let the water cascade down on me. With both palms against the cold and desolate tiled wall, I breathe in deeply trying not to cry. I think about last night and how he ruled my body, made me fall apart and lose control with him, and how I couldn't deny that I would do anything for him.

My eyes sting with tears and I squeeze them tight. Damn him. Once the burning stops, I open my eyes and grab the shower gel. Squirting it my hands, I lather it up and begin to wash my body. Caressing my breasts, I remember his tender kisses. My hand trails down between my legs washing away the slick. I'm sore, a painful reminder of what's been there. His fingers, his mouth, his...I let out a pained cry and then take deep breaths. Feeling like I've been used by the one I love is devastating. Pulling myself back together, I finish my shower and leave to get dressed. Looking in the mirror, I want to cover myself up and so I decide to go with jeans and a jumper. I look at the bed and see it's freshly made but the panties and vest are still there. I grab them and shove them right into the back of the wardrobe. I can't face them right now. I make my way down to the kitchen, and Lawrence is there. I suddenly feel full of embarrassment, because he has to know.

"Hey there, Rosannah, what do you want for breakfast?" he asks with a smile. This isn't like him; he's up to something.

"Erm, some toast?" I ask cautiously as I sit at the breakfast bar.

"Coolio." In a flash, bread is in the toaster and Lawrence hasn't appeared to move. A smirk spreads across his face. I watch as Raphael enters the kitchen. Our eyes meet and every muscle in my body feels like it's turning into stone. My racing heart almost jumps into my mouth. All he can do is frown! "Ah, this has to be good." Lawrence starts to laugh. "Rosannah already looks like she's seen a ghost, oh, wait a minute!" He chuckles. The frown drops from Raphael's face.

"Shut up, Lawrence," he hisses. I gauge Lawrence, who's still laughing; he clearly has no idea that I've slept with Raphael. I sigh inwardly with relief. I couldn't bear his taunts if he knew. Raphael joins us at the breakfast bar, sitting down opposite me with a glass of blood in his hand. Did he go to the fridge? He must have! I stare at the red liquid in the glass and wonder if it's as pleasurable for him to drink my blood as it is for me to be bitten. I start to get turned on and bite my lip to distract myself. Raphael puts his glass down pulling my attention to him. Looking at me with those intense dark eyes, he grips the bar with both hands. Slightly panicked, I let my lip go.

"Grubs up," Lawrence says as he hands me my toast. I smile at him but risk a look back at Raphael, who's still staring with his hands clenching the bar.

"Raph, staring at her won't get in her panties. Get a grip, man," Lawrence says shaking his head. We both look away from each other and my eyes fall on my plate. In my peripheral, Raphael removes his hands from the bar. I sneak a look in his direction and can see the dents in the worktop from his grip of steel. Dents caused by the very same hands that are capable of inflicting the most mind-blowing pleasure. I blush at the thought and shove a big piece of toast in my mouth to hide my embarrassment. I don't risk any more looks, and once I've finished, I take my plate to the sink. Lawrence is by my side and washes it up in a flash. I smile at him, and he grins back.

Raphael is at Lawrence's side instantly with his glass. He actually growls at Raphael but washes it up, human speed. While Raphael is distracted, I can't help but look down at his crotch. I can't believe I've actually had that! I start to feel hot and I begin to throb and moisten at the memory. I take a sharp breath in and look up. Raphael is looking straight at me. Damn it! I freeze as he raises a questioning eyebrow at me.

"So, when are we sorting out this meeting?" asks an oblivious Lawrence, tearing Raphael's attention away from me. Glad to be free from his gaze, I run off and head out into the garden through the French doors in the Hall room. I need to be alone with all these thoughts whirling around in my head.

I spend the whole day outside in the sunshine, knowing that no one will bother me out here. Although they can all walk in the sun, they're not particularly fond of it and it would raise suspicions if Raphael came out here. He would only risk it if I ran for it. I walk around the flower beds and the fountains as I ponder over Raphael. He's been acting as though nothing has happened. My mind torments me with a million different reasons as to why. The one that seems to stick in my mind is that he got an itch that he couldn't scratch and just used me to alleviate it. I'm strangely pleased that no one else knows, especially Lawrence. He'd torment us literally forever. Even at my grave, he'd torment me over it.

I move around the garden, sometimes sheltering in the shade, watching the birds dancing in the sky and on the grass and singing beautiful melodies. Putting on a little show, just for me. I smile at them and whistle back. A few of the birds risk a competition to see which one can hop the closest. A little yellow, black, and white one hops close, nodding its little head, tweeting away, and then dashes off. Then a little blue and black one dares to get closer. They take it in turns while I smile and stay very still, egging them on in my mind as they get closer and closer. The blue one wins by risking a jump onto my limp hand that lay on the dry, short lawn. I burst out laughing and both birds launch into the sky. Laying back out, I laugh at the clouds. White cotton wool and candy floss moving across a sea of bright blue. It's not long before I fall into a peaceful slumber. I'm in the bedroom, laid in bed. The moonlight streams in through one window, illuminating the bed like a spotlight.

"I'm coming for you," a male voice whispers from the dark corners of the room. I sit up and pull the covers up to my chin.

"Raphael? Is that you?" I ask, hopeful. A tall, dark figure moves forward and steps into the moonlight. His face on show for me, a face I have never seen before. He has auburn hair and dazzling grey eyes. He shakes his head as he stalks forward. He climbs onto the bed and crawls towards me. He pulls the covers from my hands.

"No, it's not Raphael." His eyes shimmer, captivating me. He nods and I expose my neck to him. In a flash, he's at my neck and bites hard. I wake with a start, bolting upright and grabbing my throat I gasp for air. I look at the sky and darkness is beginning to settle all around me. I get the feeling I'm being watched. I look at the house and see a figure standing in a top floor window. My breath catches and the figure disappears. I jump up, still puzzled about my dream. Heart pounding, I run back to the house. As I enter the hallway, I can hear a heated discussion. Curiosity gets the better of me and I walk towards the kitchen.

"Ah, the M. I. A. comes back," Lawrence calls out. I walk in to see Raphael is there, too. "Is it normal for a human's heart to race as much as yours does? I have long forgotten mine," Lawrence puzzles. I look at Raphael. My cheeks burn and dark foreboding eyes cause me to look away.

"I just fancied some sun and fresh air," I say with a sigh, ignoring Lawrence's question.

"Of course, you did." He smiles raising an eyebrow, and I sweetly smile back. Raphael lets out a low, quiet growl. I shoot him a look that asks 'what the hell' but he just goes to the fridge. I sit down at the bar where a plate of food appears in front of me.

"Thanks." I giggle at Lawrence, who's now sat next to me. Raphael sits opposite, and my laughter fades. I start eating and Lawrence decides to continue his questions, much to Raphael's dislike.

"So, you're human?" he asks straight-faced. He has to be kidding me, right?

"Well, I was the last time I checked," I say sarcastically. Raphael huffs. I ignore him, shovelling food into my mouth.

"So, you only live a hundred years when we live forever?" Lawrence quizzes. He already knows this; he's on a wind-up, great. I look at Raphael, who shifts in irritation. I swallow my mouthful to answer Lawrence.

"Eighty-five, on average. Those who make it to the one hundred mark and still have all their marbles are considered lucky." I frown looking back down at my food. I only manage a few minutes of eating in silence before Lawrence pipes back up again.

"So, you humans only last two minutes during sex?" I choke on my food causing Lawrence to slap my back excessively hard.

"Stop, stop," I manage to get out. I grab the bar with both hands in irritation. "Of all the things about humans, that's the one bit you know?" I practically growl, sucking in much-needed deep breaths. His face lights up.

"So, it's true?" he asks with glee.

"What? No! That's none of your damn business! I meant the vampire version of the Heimlich manoeuvre!" I shout. He just laughs. I scowl at my plate as I finish my food. I can see out of the corner of my eye that Lawrence is still staring at me with a smile on his face. He has more. "Go on, then," I say looking at my empty plate. He almost squeals but holds himself together.

"I'm dying to know, what's it like being human?" he asks turning his whole body to face me. Laughing, I turn to look at him. He's so silly, and it's quite adorable sometimes. He's been a vampire for so long that he's forgotten what it's like to be human.

"Well, we're not as fast as you, nor as strong," I say feeling Raphael's gaze bore into the side of my face. I look down and start to fiddle with my fingers. "We're quite emotional, and we can get easily distracted. Our time on this earth is short so we try to treasure every moment we can. We try to learn from our mistakes and make life as smooth as possible. We're scared of many things; life, death," I pause and sigh, "love. We breathe air and drink fluids. Some of us eat meat, but we all eat plants. We can't go without them for too long. Otherwise, we'll die. We're a lot more fragile than you are. We are but small on the face of the earth." I look up at Lawrence, who looks riveted.

"Fascinating, but that's incredibly boring." He frowns.

"You don't have to worry about that. You'll never be human again." I laugh as I get up from my seat and make my way over to the sink. Lawrence is there in a flash.

"It's pretty neat having one here, though. You're almost like a pet." He grins, taking the plate from me.

Raphael growls. "I'm only joking," he says with a cheeky grin.

"Well, I'm going to go to bed. I'm pretty tired," I say feeling Raphael's eyes on me as I leave the kitchen.

CHAPTER TWENTY-SEVEN

Raphael

If Lawrence weren't already dead, I would have killed him at least three times today. First, when I caught him and Nicholas in Rosannah's room. It had been quiet in the house for a few hours, but then I heard them snickering. This can only mean the pair of them are up to no good. I followed the sound to Rosannah's room and the scene that greeted me is one I never want to see again. Nicholas was sat on Rosannah's bed surrounded by her underwear while Lawrence paraded around in a silky white bra and panties. For his own sake, he was damned lucky he was still wearing his clothes! "What the hell are you doing?" I exclaimed. Turning on the spot, he held his hands out in front of me.

"Strike a pose," he said sucking in his cheeks.

"Get out of her clothes, now!" I growled. He had them off and all of the underwear away in split seconds.

"Come on, it's just a laugh. She's outside, she'll never know," Nicholas said.

"I know!" I growled.

"No need to get anal about it just because the only time you've seen Rosannah's underwear has been on me!" laughed Lawrence.

"What are you all doing in here?" asked Evangeline, who had just emerged from her room. The twins use this distraction to flee.

"Saved by you, again," I said grudgingly as I left and went back to my room.

The second time was when he refused to leave the kitchen when I wanted to talk to Rosannah.

"Hello, brother of mine," he greeted me. I could see that he was cooking.

"I want you out of here," I stated.

"I think I'll stay." He grinned.

"Why can't you just leave?" I asked.

"And miss you two together? Not a chance," he smirked. My anger boiled up, and he looked at the door knowingly.

"Ah, the M. I. A. comes back," he called, smirking at me.

The third time was when he the audacity to ask that bloody question!

"So, you humans only last two minutes during sex?" he had asked with such glee. He knows full well what humans are like, he's had enough of them! "So, it's true?" he had persisted.

"What? No! That's none of your damn business! I meant the vampire version of the Heimlich manoeuvre!" Rosannah had shouted in reply. In all fairness, it felt pretty good watching her let him have it, but it just brushed right off of his thick skin. Every time she wasn't looking, I glared at him but this only spurred him on. Amongst all of this, though, was one defining moment. Her answer to his final question. I sat rooted to the spot, taking in every word. Not daring for one second to take my eyes off her face. Lawrence, of course, had to mess that up!

"Fascinating, but that's incredibly mundane," he said.

"You don't have to worry about that. You'll never be human again," she assured him, and she was right. There's no way to reverse the transition. Too much damage is done to be able to come back to life. The heart completely gives up and over time shrivels to the size of a walnut. It never beats again once it's struck its last beat. The lungs shrink to a quarter of their size. The transition mostly destroys our digestive system, and we have no bodily fluids apart from blood and saliva.

We are not just confined to physical changes but mental ones, too. After we became accustomed to being vampires and the novelty had worn off, we went through a massive depressive state. Trying to end our existence in as many ways as we could muster. Nothing worked. Gashes, grazes, and cuts vanished before our very eyes. We healed so quickly that getting to the bone was quite a task. Axes and bullets immediately expel from our bodies. And if anything did manage the arduous chore of getting to the bone, our skeletons were so reinforced that we couldn't be dismembered, even by our own kind. We can bleed a little if we get a vein. We have to be able to make others, but that in itself is pointless as none of us can die. We're a population that either stands still or grows. It never shrinks. Hence the law against unlawful changing. We are indestructible and when we came to that realisation, we searched for a reversal. At one point, the search for it consumed us as we scoured the earth. Our greed for life dictated us rather than common sense. We went to the point of madness and beyond—breaking through the other side and coming out content. There was no going back. Once we accepted that we would live forever, and we could do nothing about it, life became much more bearable. Much more enjoyable. It became who we were as soon as we realised that once dead, always dead.

CHAPTER TWENTY-EIGHT

Rosannah

Ready for bed, I pull back the covers and see a lovely new fresh sheet. Using the power of deduction, only Raphael could have changed them. I climb in and lay down. The bed feels sparse and empty without him. I'm lost—in an endless ocean, floating in solitude with nothing but my heavy heart. I know that I'm completely and utterly in love with him. Consumed by it. Every ounce of my being screams it. It's the only reason I let him in. Well, I say let. The urge won over fighting him off. I feel wretched about it. I should have stuck to my guns, but I wanted it as much as he did.

But he didn't feel the same way as he would have stayed. I've been used, another way for him to torture me. It hits me like a ton of bricks again, and I feel winded. I gasp and close my eyes to the pain as it spreads across my chest. No matter what he does to me, I can't let him see how much this hurts. I'm broken from my thoughts when my door opens and closes. Now really isn't the time to see anyone. I open my eyes and sit up to see Raphael standing by the door with tears brimming in my eyes and threatening to spill down my cheeks. Don't want him to see how much it hurts? Fail.

That look plays in his eyes, and I can tell what he's here for. He won't use me again. I feel my pulse race, and I fill with anger. Leaving the bed, I stalk towards him. "I don't know what you think you're doing but you can get out," I grate at him. His top lip curls up, and he flashes his teeth. I stop dead, deciding not get any closer but still my rant flows. "It happened once but it won't again. I know this has been just a little game for you, and you just love to torment me, but I'd no longer like to take part," I say trying not to let my voice waver and trying to ignore the fire in his eyes. He's at me in a split second pulling me to him and pressing his lips against my ear. Grabbing my hand, he shoves it against his crotch.

"Does this feel like a game to you?" he hisses in my ear. "Because I can assure you that it's not." I can feel his very hard erection against the palm of my hand. I swallow the lump of emotion in my throat and fight with all my strength against the urge to shove my hand down his jeans and take him in my palm. I can't believe how bold my desire is making me behave. He doesn't understand that it's still a game if it's only about him getting off. I pull back to get some distance and see two jet black eyes.

"It's always a game when there are no emotions involved," I scathe, tears filling my eyes and turning my view abstract. He lightly hisses and releases me, causing me to stagger back a couple of steps. "I'm not some floozy. Plenty of them out there would gladly give you what you want, but instead, you choose me for your own sick reasons. I bared.... God, I let you...Because I..." I can't bring myself to say the words. Not to him, not aloud. Raphael grabs my shoulders as I fail to stop the tears from falling.

"Because you what, Rosannah? Because you what?" he demands. He then sighs in exasperation when I don't answer. "You think I used you? Is that it?" He runs his hands down his face. He grabs my face and looks deep into my eyes. His eyes are back to their light milky grey. "Listen, Rosannah," he murmurs with a worried expression. "I..." He's cut off.

"Damn Raphael, leave the poor girl alone. If she doesn't want your goods, you've got to leave her be." We both look at a smirking Lawrence, who's opened the door and is leaning into the room. He chuckles and disappears. Raphael looks back to my expectant face.

"Ah, right. Well, I shall leave you to it," he says before also disappearing.

"Raphael!" I yell after him. Damn Lawrence and damn you! I get back in bed and fall into a dreamless slumber.

Once I wake up, I have my daily shower, get dressed, and race downstairs. I'm desperate to speak to Raphael, but I find that everyone is in the kitchen. Damn. Raphael looks at me and smiles. Damn you even more! I smile a tight grin at him.

"Right, Missy, you're heading out with me to find an outfit for this evening. You're going to look fabulous!" Evangeline beams.

"Wait a minute, what?" I ask her puzzled.

"You know The Synod is coming over tonight, right? It's our monthly meeting. You have to look your best and that means going shopping." She smiles a friendly smile at me. I flick a look at Raphael and back to Evangeline feeling panic rise. I've thrown on a smart dress to go to my work's Christmas meal, but that's as far as I go regarding dressing up. It's bad enough being the only human here, never mind wearing anything that says look at me, vampire bait right here.

"Why do I have to dress up?" I whisper, frowning.

"Oh, like you don't enjoy getting dolled up," Evangeline says confidently. "Right, let's go and shop," she squeaks, clapping her hands together. She grabs my arm and pulls me out of the kitchen, literally dragging me into the garage and into a car. Wow, there are cars here. I look at my poor Anthea just sat there. We drive for hours down country lanes passing the occasional farmhouse that time has forgotten all about. Winding our way through fields, we eventually hit our destination. A very large underground shopping centre.

"What is this place?" I queried.

"It's a vampire shopping centre. Whatever you do, keep your mouth shut. No matter what," she warned me before we got out of the car. Yes, amazingly they exist. An odd place full of pale skin and light grey eyes. Every so often, a vampire would compliment Evangeline on her livestock. I had to bite my tongue on several occasions. Evangeline dragged me around every shop, at least, three times. My feet were killing me, but we eventually found some outfits. We arrive back at the house a few hours later and grabbing the bridge of my nose, I walk into the entertaining room where everyone else is.

"Please don't ever let me go shopping with your sister again. She's a bloody machine," I say completely exhausted.

"Oh, it wasn't that bad." She laughs as she pops up behind me, making me jump and yelp. I stomp over to the other side of the room. Exasperated, I sigh, collapsing on a lonely seat that's against the far wall.

"Yes, it was. I never want to visit another shop for as long as I live," I complain. Lawrence and Nicholas laugh in unison, and I scowl at them. I then look around and realise Raphael isn't here. Everyone starts talking to each other and I tune out. I lean my head back against the wall and close my eyes. I wonder where he is. I sigh and open my eyes sitting up. I jump and yelp, bringing my knees up. All the others have gone and there's just Raphael standing there, dead in front of me with his arms crossed. "Oh, you made me jump," I say breathlessly, blinking at him and taking in the view. My heart throbs in my throat, and I'm breathing heavily as I slowly set my feet back down on the floor.

"I love hearing you make those noises," he says through gritted teeth. I gasp as all my muscles clench tightly. He drops to his knees in front of me. Pinning me with his gaze, I watch helplessly as he grabs my knees and pulls them apart. I lean back and put my hands either side of the seat to steady myself. He runs his hands up my thighs and grabs my ass. Squeezing it hard, he pulls me forward and rams his face between my legs, taking in my scent. He growls and I arch my back moaning, pushing my hips forward. Suddenly, he's gone. I sit up and blink fast. What the hell? Nicholas appears in the doorway.

"You all right?" He pulls a funny face. "I heard some odd sounds coming from in here," he says looking confused.

"Oh, it was nothing. Nothing at all. As usual," I scathe getting up and stomping past him. I pass Lawrence and Evangeline, who both looked equally as puzzled. How did he bypass all of them? Who cares.

"I'll be up soon to help you get ready," she calls after me as I retreat to my room. How could they not have heard all of that? They're completely oblivious! Unless they just put it down to Raphael's sexual frustration. Unbeknown to them, a frustration I've helped to alleviate! In no time at all, Evangeline's knocking at the door. Wow, that would be a first!

"Come in," I yell. My smile fades when Raphael walks in instead. He goes to say something but Evangeline interrupts.

"Raph, she's not interested. Get out and go masturbate or something." I can hear the twins laughing in unison from down the hall. Raphael looks horrified and promptly leaves. Damn it! I'll never get it out of him with this lot! "Ask the twins, they'll give you tips," she yells as she walks to the door. The twins immediately stop laughing.

"Hey!" they yell as she slams the door.

"Right, get in the shower and pull on the underwear we bought. Then come out here and I'll fix the rest." She smiles.

I grab the bag that houses the barely-there underwear and head into the bathroom, closing the door behind me. Turning the shower on, I strip and turn my attention to the bag's contents. I pull the small wad of mint lace and silk from it. There's a balcony bra with incredibly thin straps. It will apparently give me a bust Dolly Parton would envy.

The bottom half of the cups are paneled silk joined by a border of woven ribbon to the top half, which is mint lace. The lace is flowery and intricately decorated with silver embroidery. It has a scalloped edge, which is dotted silver and mint diamantes. A small bow sits sweetly between the cups. I remove the tags and set it next to the sink. I then look at the next garment. It's the matching G-string. The front panel is lace, which is silver and mint like the bra. There's paneled silk on the sides and undercarriage. There are diamantes running along the front edge with another delicate bow in the middle and the back thins out and lays flat running into a fragile strap of elasticated ribbon. I hold it up looking at it. It looks so uncomfortable. Just like dental floss. I remove the tags, lay it next to the bra, and then pull out the next item. It's the matching suspender belt. It's a pure paneled silk and gathers up in the middle with another bow and a diamante border along the top. It has four straps with grippers on them.

"Hurry up in there!" Evangeline yells. I yelp and put down the suspender belt and literally dive into the shower and start scrubbing. Once I'm done, I get out and dry myself off. Wrapping my hair in a towel, I pick up the suspender belt and remove the tags. I still can't believe Evangeline got these. According to her, no one will see any underwear lines and it will show off my awesome breasts and ass. She asked me what size I was and was pretty amazed when I said a 32D. I usually hide them away as best as I can. Evangeline had jumped for joy because I'd be able to pull off a balcony bra. She said it would drive Raphael insane. I nearly died when the thought of Raphael seeing me in this entered my head. When she spotted my embarrassment, she told me not to be so stupid because only she who would actually see me in it when she helped me get ready. I put all the underwear on and looked in the mirror. I gasp when I catch a glimpse of my breasts. They're huge! Evangeline wasn't kidding. I reach in the bag for the last items. Skin coloured silk stockings. I try to clip them up, but I have no chance. No matter how hard I squeeze, I can't clip them shut.

I take them off and walk out into the bedroom to Evangeline wolf whistling at me. "Look at those bad boys!" she says with raised eyebrows.

"Yeah, yeah, help me with these," I say in exasperation, holding up the stockings. She grabs them from me and I hold onto her as she threads them one at a time onto my feet and up my legs. In a flash, she's clipped them up. To my horror, the door opens and I shoot a glance over there.

"Hey, Evangeline, do you know where...Whoa, damn, you look hot!" Lawrence gushes. Nicholas pops his head around, too.

"Whoa," he agrees mouth open.

"Get out, now!" Evangeline shouts at them. They slam the door shut and she huffs.

"Filthy little pervs," she mutters. "Right, arms up." I lift my arms and the dress is on me in an instant. I drop my arms and walk over to the mirror. The dress, which is beautiful, boasts the same colour as the underwear. Mint green. It's a bodycon stretchy lace dress with long sleeves that have a scalloped edge. The neckline is a v shape that's scalloped, too, with my breasts bulging out of the top. There's a sewn-in slip made of stretchy silk that blocks anyone's views of my body. The dress is tight and clings to every part of my body ending just above my knees with another scalloped edge. With my hair in rollers, Evangeline then spent minutes doing my makeup. The makeup was neutral, enhancing my natural beauty. She made me laugh when she told me that she didn't want me to look like a whore. "I'll be back in ten minutes." She smiles as she pops out. The twins were still out there trying to get another look.

"Urgh, bugger off you two. Ah, guests are arriving, go and greet them. We'll be down in about fifteen minutes," she chastises them.

"Okay," they sulk. After a while, Evangeline comes back, and she's all ready. She's wearing a pink tight long satin halter-neck dress that has a small slit up the right leg. The dress has no embroidery or patterns. It's just plain, but she's paired it with extremely sparkly pink high heel sandals and huge chandelier earrings and matching necklace. Her hair is high up in a large sock bun and she has thick eyeliner and loads of eyelashes.

"You look lovely." I smile at her.

"Thank you. Let's get this hair finished." She grins. Ten minutes later, I have large, voluminous curls cascading around my shoulders. She's gone with mermaid hair for me. I'm in high platform mint green patented heels. Luckily, for me, I can actually walk in them! Evangeline's pretty impressed.

"So, what are these meetings about?" I ask before we leave the room.

"They just discuss any issues." She smiles.

"Me being the current issue." I frown.

"Don't be silly. They know you're okay here." She smiles. I put on a smile but worry niggles at me. She holds out her hand, and arm in arm, we head off downstairs together.

CHAPTER TWENTY-NINE

Raphael

"Filthy little pervs," I hear Evangeline yell.

"Up to no good again," I mutter to myself.

"And we're here to tell you all about it," Lawrence says as I realise the twins are both behind me. I turn to face them.

"What have you two done now?" I ask suspiciously.

"Only seen Rosannah in her underwear." Lawrence grins. If blood flowed through my veins, I would have felt the colour drain from my face.

"You did what?" I manage to get out.

"We popped our heads into Rosannah's room to ask Evangeline about something, and we got an eyeful of Rosannah in some skimpy lingerie!" exclaims Nicholas.

"My God, those curves!" Lawrence drools.

"Yeah, she could definitely be a pinup," says Nicholas.

"Definitely D's," he says to Lawrence. I feel the anger rising in me. Only I should get to see her like that! I know it was an accident, but I'm enraged!

"Whoa, we best get out of here. He looks like he's about to blow," says a serious Nicholas.

"Plus, we want to get another glimpse of Rosannah's fine body." Lawrence laughs, and they disappear. I want to chase after them, but the sound of guests arriving stops me. I race down and open the door before they knock. A vampire never knocks on the door of another vampire's house. We can hear if they're in, and they can hear us arrive. Knocking is polite, but we've grown accustomed to skipping it.

"Raphael," greets Mathias.

"This is Maria, my wife." He smiles. In all the years I've known The Synod, I have never met their respected other halves. This gets my back up. I take her hand and plant a very light kiss on it.

"Please go through to the entertaining room." I smile. "Ah, Porticus." I smile.

"I'd like you to meet Franklin." He wraps an arm around the waist of a very hench Latino looking male vampire. I wouldn't have put Porticus as gay. It comes as a shock to me as I thought I knew him very well.

"Nice to meet you," I say as I shake his hand. They walk off to the entertaining room. A solo Bernadette gives a fleeting smile as she walks past me to join the others. She's not one for pleasantries.

"Raphael."

"Reggie," I retort. He's on his own. I know for a fact that he's married, but he walks off before I can question where his wife is. Vladimir is the last guest to turn up. He's accompanied by a busty blonde. She's literally nothing but tits and very long platinum blonde hair, but surprisingly, she's human.

"I'd like you to meet Cindy," he says as he grabs her ass and pulls her in close. She squeals in delight.

"Lovely to meet you," she says as she holds her hand out to me. I give it a light kiss on the back. "Follow me," I say as I lead them to the entertaining room. "Right, can we get to business before we all settle?" I ask the room.

"Certainly," Reggie agrees as he steps forward. "We think Rosannah should be turned," he sneers.

"She most certainly will not be," I say. A few gasps jump around the room.

"Well, it's fortunate that we're against that then, isn't it," Mathias says glaring at him.

"Any real concerns?" I ask the room.

"It's come to our attention that there was a break-in here," Mathias says cautiously. I knew it wouldn't be long before The Synod found out.

"It was dealt with and won't happen again."

"But the intruder came here knowing Rosannah was here," says Reggie.

"Like I said, it was dealt with." I glare at him.

"How about we forget about this and just enjoy ourselves?" asks a nervous Mathias.

"I couldn't have put it better myself. Please help yourselves to glasses of blood on the tables," I tell everyone. I know this is done for now, but it certainly is far from over. Reggie has a bee in his bonnet, and for some stupid reason, Mathias always entertains him. I wander over to Porticus. I'm still wary of him. I know he was acting in everyone's best interest, but he still voted against me. I don't really want him talking to Rosannah, but there's not a lot I can do about that. "Porticus, I had no idea," I say putting on a smile.

"That I was gay?" he asks seriously.

"Yes."

"Neither did I." He laughs looking over at Franklin, who's talking to the twins. "I had no idea how much better things would be with a male vampire. If I had known so many years ago, I would have tried it in my human life." He smiles.

"Well, I'm glad you're h..." Porticus nudges my arm midsentence and nods quickly to the door. My head turns in the direction he's indicating to see the most beautiful sight.

CHAPTER THIRTY

Rosannah

We enter the entertaining room, and there are plenty of vampires in there. They all turn to look at us and smile except a white-haired blonde who's still nattering away. All the others are big grins and light grey eyes. It's nice to see that they're happy and not angry, horny, or hungry. That, so far, is what I've concluded the black eyes are about. The deeper the shade, the stronger the feeling.

I look over to the other side of the room and spot Raphael. He's deep in conversation with Porticus. It gives me a good opportunity to well, check him out. He's dressed in a tailored black suit with a very dark plain red shirt, complementing it all with a black silk tie. The dark red and his pale skin are quite a breath-taking combination, and he certainly looks incredible in a suit. Now I can see why Brianna goes on about suits. Porticus realises that everyone has stopped talking and is now looking at Evangeline and me. I guess these vampires stop to stare at anyone who enters the room. Porticus lightly nudges Raphael, who suddenly stops talking and snaps his head to look right at me. We lock eyes with each other as the other vampires continue with idle chitchat. Porticus continues chatting to him while he just stares at me. His looks have the power to command anyone who lays eyes on his face to gawk at him, not me. He then flashes me a cheeky smile while Porticus isn't looking, and I imagine him in all his naked glory. Ah, crap. I knew this would happen. I break from his gaze to quickly grab a glass from a small batch on the table next to me and go to swig it.

"Wait!" says a worried Evangeline, who grabs my arm with one hand and takes the glass with the other. She sniffs the glass and lets out a huge sigh of relief. "Yes, it's wine." She smiles, handing the glass back to me and releasing my arm. I watch her go as she wanders off to mingle. Astounding. Even I can tell the difference between blood and wine, Evangeline! I take a few big mouthfuls, and the contents are gone. I feel it burn its way down to my stomach. Surprised that I didn't gag, I swap my empty glass for another full one and then head for a solitary chair I've spotted tucked out of the way. I can feel eyes on my back, but when I turn to sit, everyone's engrossed in conversation.

I wile some time away watching them all. It honestly looks like extreme speed dating. Chatting for a few minutes then whizzing off to someone else. Glasses vanishing from the tables. I look at where I got mine. There are seven glasses there. Jeez! How much do they expect me to drink! I'm not shy of a glass or two, but that's too much! While looking at the glasses, the blonde walks over and grabs a glass. I'm incredibly shocked to see that she's human. Her piercing blue eyes are an obvious giveaway. From that point on, I'm desperate to speak to her, but I'm not going to flounce over to her. The occasional vampire comes and speaks to me. Asking me about my human life and reminiscing about theirs. Raphael chooses to just watch me from the other side of the room. Catching my gaze every so often with eyes a slightly cloudy dark grey. He seems quite content until Porticus comes to talk to me. He's been dying to talk to me all night, according to Evangeline. She tells me bits and bobs as she pops over every now and then to see how I'm doing.

"Well, I can see that Raphael has done a wonderful job with you." He smiles. If only you knew the truth, unless you do know? I flush a little at the thought.

"Oh, yes, he has. He's looked after me quite well." I force a smile while taking a quick glance at Raphael. No longer carefree and relaxed, his shoulders are slightly hunched and his eyes sharp. Why would talking to Porticus have his back up? I make a mental note to ask Evangeline later.

"Maybe I was wrong about my vote." He sighs. Ah, of course. He voted against Raphael. How could I forget that?

"Well, you were being honest and voted for what you thought was best. I got to stay anyway, so it's not like you caused any problems." I smile.

"You are a very sweet girl." He looks at his watch. "Oh right, I've got more mingling to do; it was lovely to see you again." He grabs my hand and kisses the back of it. His lips ice cold against the warmth of my skin. I'm a little taken aback by the gesture but put a smile on my face for when he looks back up at me. He glides back to one of the vampires I haven't seen before this evening. Franklin. Easy on the eye but incredibly flamboyant. I peek at Raphael, who looks pissed off. I pull a face of slight distaste and shrug my shoulders slightly as his face smooths out into a small smile. I see Evangeline talking to the busty blonde who looks over and smiles at me. She strides over on long pin legs, exposed by her incredibly short mini dress. It's a lovely lilac colour, but with her breasts trying to escape the top and the hem bordering dangerously close to her panties, it's not a flattering look on her. I have lost count of how many times I've seen her panties this evening. The twins have been snickering about it, but everyone else has been respectful. Alex's words spring to mind. Vampire wannabe. Or vampire bait! The busty blonde reaches me and pulls a chair over to sit next to me.

"I'm Cindy." She smiles sweetly at me. I can see from her eyebrows that she certainly isn't a natural blonde. Underneath her caked on make-up, I can see she's not much younger than me. She's dripping in what I can only assume are diamonds.

"I'm Rosannah." I smile back.

"Oh, I know who you are," she says knowingly. I look at her enviously. Not because she's the reincarnation of Barbie, but because she doesn't appear to be under lock and key.

"Are you free to roam?" I ask.

"Well, I've been there, but it's certainly not free." She laughs. Oh, wow. Someone worse than Evangeline.

"Who are you here with?" I ask trying not to show my disbelief.

"Vlad." She smiles. I smile at her endearing name for him. The way she lights up, I think she's really in love with him. I stand corrected. Vampire lover, not vampire wannabe.

"Are you Vlad's prisoner?" I ask.

"Only in the bedroom." She giggles. I hear the twins snigger quietly. I look around the room. No one's looking, but I know they can all hear us. "Oh, sweetie, now I know what you mean. Silly me." She slaps my right knee. The twins snigger again. I shoot them a look, and they stop. Cindy's completely oblivious. "I've been brainwashed not to tell anyone who isn't a vampire about vampires." She grins flashing perfect white teeth at me. I'm so intrigued by her relationship.

"Why vampire instead of human?" I ask.

"Well, he's absolutely gorgeous. It was his looks and those eyes that caught my attention," she gushes.

"It was love at first sight. He asked me out, but I said no. I have been out with so many jerks that I thought Vlad would just be another one, but he's such a gentleman. He was so persistent, and I eventually said yes. We had dated for some time before he told me that he was a vampire. He was worried that I wouldn't accept it. He brainwashed me first into not being able to tell anyone who doesn't know about vampires. If I didn't like it, he was going to brainwash me into forgetting he'd told me anything. But once he told me, I was completely fine with it and the brainwashing stopped there." She smiles looking over to Vlad fondly who was talking to Porticus.

"Plus, the sex is amazing!" she gushes. The twins, who have been creeping around chatting to each other, are listening to every word. "You really should try it!" She grins. The twin's heads turn very slowly to look at us. Eyebrows raised they just stand and stare. I quickly glance past them to Raphael. His dark grey eyes flash to mine, and I look away feeling flushed with embarrassment. "I'm going to get back to my Vlad." She smiles and makes her way over to

Vlad. Dropping her clutch purse on the way, she bends over to pick it up. Fortunately, the twins whip behind her blocking my view. As she straightens up, Lawrence makes his way over to me. "Dance with me," he says holding his left hand out to me.

"There's no music!" I protest.

"There is in my head," he says with a wiggle of his eyebrows.

"Come on," he coaxes. "Or I'll cause a scene," he sings with a smirk. I know it's not an empty threat.

"Okay, okay. I'll dance with you," I say begrudgingly, getting up and taking his hand. Placing my free hand on his left shoulder, he grabs my waist and pulls me in close. We start to sway, and I feel ridiculous. Not only are we the only couple dancing, but we're also dancing to no music! Only Lawrence. I bury my face in the nape of his neck too scared to glance at Raphael. I feel a whisk of movement, and when I look up, we're right at the bottom of the garden. There's no one but the stars and us.

"So, what did you think of Barbie's panties being strangled by her ass cheeks?" he asks deadly serious. I burst out laughing. His rock hard arms hold solid, keeping me within their boundaries. "Seriously, they were screaming for help," he says.

"Thank goodness you and Nicholas blocked my view," I say catching my breath.

"You know, Nicholas and I had a bet who could get you to dance. I won," he says with a triumphant grin. I quietly giggle as we sway for a small while. A tap on Lawrence's shoulder stops us in our tracks. Expecting it to be Raphael, I'm surprised to see it's Nicholas.

"Can I cut in?" he asks giving Lawrence a light growl. Lawrence looks a little concerned but moves away to allow Nicholas to take over.

Something is wrong here and my skin crawls as he works a hand around my back. It's a little too low and his fingers lightly massage. I stiffen up, and my heart throbs in my ears. "I want to talk to you on your own." He's looking so intensely at me. I watch as Lawrence enters the house. "Ignore him," he says. My heart kicks up a notch, this certainly doesn't feel right at all. He looks into my eyes. "Kiss me," he coos. I stare at him wide-eyed. We look at one another in silence for a moment. "Oh, come on. I'm only joking. Your face is hilarious," he says laughing, letting go of me. This is really freaking me out.

"It's not funny," I say.

"Okay, okay. Sorry. Come here." He reaches out and pulls me back into dance. "I just wanted to get away from everyone. It was getting too claustrophobic in there, and it's all too serious for me. Although, I could watch Barbie all night." He grins.

"You know, the way you and your brother act, anyone would think you were both frustrated," I say disgusted by his objectism. He pulls me in even closer.

"Want to be another notch on my bedpost? Help out a probable cause?" he smirks, raising his eyebrows at me.

"No, definitely not." I shake my head.

"Relax, I'm joking. Again. I can assure you that I am never frustrated, the numbers go into the thousands." He grins.

"Urgh, thanks for telling me that," I huff. He chuckles.

"So, when are you going to give it to Raphael?" he asks a little too sternly for my liking. I ignore him. "Ah, so you're keeping your game plan to yourself," he contemplates with a nod.

"I don't have a game plan because I'm not playing any games. Besides, your brother doesn't play fair at all," I say knowing that I've already given Raphael what he wants. Nicholas turns deathly serious.

"Have you ever thought that us vampires might just have a problem expressing our feelings?" Whoa.

"If you're referring to Raphael, I don't think he has any idea what it's like to really like anyone," I scoff.

"Well, he was quite taken with Emily, but you know what happened there. He vowed never to let himself fall in love. It's quite tragic, really. He's emotionally scarred and won't let anyone in," he explains, staring up at the night's sky. This really irks me. I have a feeling he's trying to wind me up for whatever reason but if the shoe fits. I decide not to rise to the bait.

"So, have you ever been in love?" I quiz him. He looks conflicted. After a moment, he answers.

"No. Humans have an obvious downfall, and most vampires are assholes," he says looking away from me.

"So, humans are a no go?" I ask intrigued. I hope he says yes.

"Of course. No one wants to watch someone they care about waste away and die. It's one of the pitfalls of being immortal." He frowns. I forget how long the Monstrums have been on this earth, and that they will continue to be here long after I'm dead. Nicholas stops dancing and bows while I curtsey. "Thank you for the dance," he says with a forlorn smile and dashes off leaving me alone outside at the bottom of the garden.

Great. I stare up at the moon; it's a full one. I can't help but wonder if there are werewolves out there, too, in the big wide world. There are vampires; nothing else would surprise me now. I walk back to the house. Nicholas has well and truly freaked me out. What do I do? Tell Raphael? Surely he knows, he must have heard that? I walk into the entertaining room. Everyone has gone, apart from Reggie, who hasn't spoken to me all night.

"I suppose I should say hi to you," he sneers. I smile at him. Jerk.

"Though, I must say as much as I'm not a fan of yours, you certainly look quite ravishing tonight." He smiles.

"Well, I suppose I'll take that as a compliment. Thank you." I smile again.

He replies with another sneer. "I see the way you look at Raphael. I wouldn't bother; he can have his pick of any female vampires. He wouldn't even waste his time with you. You can't offer him anything he could possibly want. He will ruin you just for the pure fun of it. I'd advise you keep away from him," he says with slight spite.

"Well, Mr. Mastermind, that's quite a difficult task when I happen to be a prisoner in his house. Don't worry. I can't stand vampires. You're all disgusting, hideous creatures, and I'd rather die than have anything to do with any of you!" I scathe. Reggie is visibly shocked, but I leave before he has the chance to say anymore. I walk out into the hallway and bump into Evangeline.

"Is everything okay?" she asks looking quite concerned. Reggie walks past, ignoring us, making his way to Raphael, who's saying goodbye to some of the guests. My stomach knots and I just want to go to bed.

"Yeah, everything is fine." I force a smile. I see that Reggie has engaged Raphael in deep conversation. I leave Evangeline standing there and make my way up to my room.

CHAPTER THIRTY-ONE

Raphael

"It was good to see you all again," I lie.

"When will the next meeting be?" I ask Mathias.

"In a month's time at mine." He smiles. I'll find a way out of that one. "Look, Raphael. I understand that you know what you're doing, but be careful. Not all of us are as supportive as others," he says with an underlying warning. I look over at the entertaining room and can see that Reggie is talking to Rosannah. She doesn't seem too happy about it.

"I have no idea what you're talking about," I say. He gauges me for a few seconds.

"Of course, Raphael." He smiles. I force a smile as he leaves and notice Rosannah storm upstairs leaving a bewildered Evangeline standing in the middle of the hallway. I go to follow her, but Reggie stops me.

"Raphael, I am deeply concerned," he sneers. Here we go.

"Rosannah seems to be quite infatuated with you. That's a dangerous thing. It's a risk for The Synod. For you," he says seriously. For him, he means.

"And what do you suggest I do?" I ask him trying to hide my anger.

"Well, turn her over to us or change her," he says.

"It's not as easy as that," I say as my fists clench by my sides.

"Surely, it is. The Synod does not want to be compromised and think it best she was no longer a problem," he says.

"Really? So, which one of you is lying, then?" I ask. He straightens up.

"Them, of course. They will tell you whatever you want to hear to keep you sweet. I don't do things purely because I'm told to. You know that more than anyone else," he says clearly insulted.

"Well, you just worry about yourself like you usually do, and I'll worry about everything else," I say walking off before I do something I'll regret. I hear the door close behind me. Can I trust Reggie's word? It is typical of The Synod to lie to keep me sweet. It's happened before. They feed me bullshit. I pull out my trump card, and they are kissing my arse for weeks. I believe him. Evangeline and the twins appear in front of me.

"We're going to head off," says Evangeline. She's acting like nothing just happened.

"You're not staying?" I ask.

"There's no point. We know you're keeping clear of Rosannah, and while she's asleep, we can't wind you both up." Lawrence grins and I look at Evangeline.

"I miss my own bed." She shrugs.

"Fine, I'll see you all tomorrow, no doubt," I say as they head off.

"Nicholas, Lawrence," I call after them. Evangeline stops as they walk back. "Goodnight Evangeline," I hint. She sighs but dashes off. "Either of you want to explain the dancing and garden episode to me?" I ask. Nicholas looks off into the distance, but Lawrence pipes up.

"Just another one of our bets you know. Who could get her to dance. That's all," he says with a worried and forced grin.

"I shall tell you how it looked to me. Lawrence, you get Rosannah into the garden with your usual pathetic jokes so that Nicholas can come and take over. Once Nicholas has taken over, you then leave them alone. Nicholas then has the opportunity to try it on with Rosannah. How am I doing so far?" I ask. Nicholas glares at me, but Lawrence gives me look of shame.

"Oh, come on Raphael, it's not like you haven't tried it on with her," Nicholas says. If only he knew, but I still do not intend to tell him. Especially not now.

"He's in love with her," Lawrence tells him.

"I..."

"He's not; so what does it really matter?" Nicholas asks Lawrence. I am speechless and have no idea what to say.

"We better head off, see you tomorrow," Lawrence says with a nervous smile and pulls Nicholas with him. The door closes behind them, and it is now just Rosannah and me.

CHAPTER THIRTY-TWO

Rosannah

I head to the bed, and as I get there, the door open and closes. I huff loudly. "Whoever you are, go away. I'm not in the best of moods!" I warn. Silence. I turn to face whoever it is. "I said...Oh." It's Raphael and my heart pounds. He has that look I love so much.

"I've got to get you out of that dress. I've been hard since I first saw you in it," he growls. I suck in a deep breath as he walks over to me. The others must have gone. Grabbing both my wrists, he lifts my left hand over my head causing me to turn. "See?" he growls in my ear, pulling my crossed arms towards him and causing me to push back onto him. His very hard erection presses against the very bottom of my spine. I arch my back pushing my ass against him. He groans and releases my wrists then moves my hair out of the way. He slowly unbuttons my dress, planting soft kisses on the back of my neck. His cool lips cause my breath to catch. When he undoes the bottom one, he slides the dress off my shoulders and trails it all the way down to the floor. I am powerless against him as my desire takes over. I step out of the dress and the shoes. Still crouched behind me, he grabs my hips and kisses his way back up, nipping my ass as he passes it. Once standing, he turns me around. He groans when he sees me clad in mint silk and lace, or rather, the lack of it. "God, you look sooo hot." In a flash, his trousers and boxers are gone and his big hard erection is in his hand. He's pumping it, looking me right in the eyes. The naive part of me is prudishly embarrassed while the curious side is exhilarated. I very slowly start to unclip my stockings and slide them down my legs. Thank goodness, they're easier to take off than put on! I unhook my suspender belt and let it drop to the floor.

"The things you make me want to do," I whisper. He gasps, looking me up and down. I then turn around and undo the bra, letting it fall down my arms and to the floor. I then slowly pull down my G-string bending all the way over to take it down to my feet and stand back up. When I turn back around, he's completely naked.

"I have to have you now," he growls. He grabs me and carries me to the bed. Laying me down, he pulls my knees apart then climbs on top and kisses me as he enters me. We both groan together. I want to watch him, so I roll us over and straddle him. As I start to ride him, he reaches up for me, but I bat his hands away. They fall back above his head. I stare him straight in the eyes as I groan caressing my breasts. I slow every time an orgasm threatens so I can keep watching him. "Damn it, I want to watch you come. I need to watch you come," he begs. I can't get enough. He starts moaning, and I watch as he falls apart beneath me, his face contorting with emotion. The end of his erection rubs that tender sensitive part inside of me, making it hard to ignore. Pressing me on, pushing me higher. I whimper and climax, tensing and convulsing around him as I collapse onto his chest. He wraps his arms around me and rolls us back over. Sinking his fangs into my neck, he thrusts hard and deep. I cry out, a wicked and intoxicating mixture of pain and pleasure. My hands knead his ass as he sucks on the bite. Swirling his tongue across the wounds, he seals them off. "The taste of you, I can never get enough," he growls in my ear. The ferocity of his lovemaking soon pushes me over the edge, and we climax together. I dig my fingernails into his back as he rides the waves out. He rolls over and pulls me into his arms like he did last time. We fall asleep tangled in each other.

***

I wake in the morning, and he's gone. Again. I'm going to have this out with him! When I get dressed, I head off to find Raphael. As I exit the room, I can hear yelling. I slowly wander down the stairs, and as I get closer to the argument, I can start to make out words.

"Yeah, but I never thought you'd actually do it!" I get to the bottom of the stairs and see the back of Raphael. He's standing in the kitchen doorway. On his left is Evangeline, and on his right is Lawrence. Raphael must be arguing with Nicholas! I walk towards them in a hurry. Everything then moves in slow motion. As I reach Raphael, he flies backwards as Nicholas pushes him flying across the room. He smashes through the monster of a front door and beyond where I can see. Nicholas's eyes are pure black, and he's snarling with fangs on display. Lawrence and Evangeline grab an arm each and hold him back.

"Why would you do this to me?" he screams to Raphael, who is now making his way back into the house. I'm so confused, what has gotten into him! Raphael is then in front of Nicholas trying to calm him down. With his hands on Nicholas's shoulders, he turns to look at me.

"Get out of here!" he shouts to me. I stare at him, my mind blank. I can't take in what's happening. He suddenly shoots off and returns in the blink of an eye. Back to help calm a snarling, snapping Nicholas. He turns to me with anger in his eyes that I've never seen before. He throws my handbag at me.

"Get the fuck out of here, NOW!" he screams. I'm frightened to the core and run towards the door that leads to the garage. I turn the handle and fling the door open. Rooting through my bag, I find my keys and open Anthea. I jump in and start her up. The garage door is already open. I reverse straight out, turn around, and drive towards the gate. My heart sinks even more when I see it's already open. As I get onto the main road, tears start falling from my eyes. I can't believe what happened. Why would Nicholas be so angry? I don't even know exactly what they were arguing about. Once I get home, I race up into my flat. I'm so glad to see Marmalade but not so happy to see that my answer machine is full. Mum. I collapse onto the couch and burst into tears. Marmalade snuggles up with me as I cry my torn and shattered heart out. I never want to see any of them again.

CHAPTER THIRTY-THREE

Raphael

Luckily, I had left Rosannah's room before the others had arrived, not that it made any difference in the long run.

"Raph, you can always go back after her," says Evangeline from the study door.

"Leave, now!" I yell, not bothering to look at her. She scurries away, and I'm left to my thoughts once again. I sit in my study trying to deal with the aftermath of this morning. It keeps replaying in my mind. Like a broken record.

"You are here early," I say to Nicholas from the kitchen doorway. He is sat at the breakfast bar.

"The others are here, too." He shrugs.

"So, did you or didn't you?" asks Lawrence, who appears to my right.

"What?" I ask exasperated.

"Screw Rosannah," he smirks.

"God, what is it with you and that?" I ask beginning to get irritated. He has clearly forgotten about Nicholas and last night.

"That's not an answer." He grins.

"It's none of your business!" I yell at him.

"Well, I like to think it's mine," pipes up Nicholas.

"What?" I ask surprised. He walks over to me.

"I said, I like to think it's mine," he repeats.

226

"I heard you the first time. I do not see how it is any of your business, either," I say.

"I'm in love with her," he declares.

"You've got to be kidding me!" I yell at the ceiling.

"Oh, don't act like you didn't know!" he yells back. Evangeline appears on my left.

"Did I just hear right?" she asks.

"Shut up, Evangeline," we all say in unison. I shoot a look at Lawrence, who looks at the floor. So he knew about all of this?

"That still does not make it any of your business," I tell Nicholas.

"It is when I am trying to court her," he says with a light growl.

"Trying to court her? Does she even know?" I ask Nicholas trying not to laugh. His eyes grow darker.

"You worried about the competition? You've been nothing but nasty, evil, and malicious to her. When I tell her how I feel, she'll flock to me!" he says with a viciousness lacing his words.

"She would not even kiss you when you asked. If you think she will come running to you, then you're delusional!" I spit.

"Oh, you want to talk about delusional? Delusional is you being in love with her thinking that she'd ever be interested in you! Twice you've been alone with her here for the whole night and she hasn't so much as sniffed in your direction! Mine and Lawrence's bets have been nothing but an utter joke. Why the hell would she fuck you?!" he yells. I close my eyes and force my rage back down. Opening my eyes, I look him straight in the eyes.

"I can assure you that I have done much more than that to her," I say calmly.

"Whoa, Raph!" blurts out Lawrence.

"He's lying," Nicholas says, his eyes fixed on mine.

"How do you know?" asks a shocked Evangeline.

"Of course, he's lying. She's not that easy, or stupid," he answers. His eyes still trained on mine.

"Both times, all night," I say, telling the truth. I watch as it sinks in.

"How could you?" he asks visibly upset.

"How was I supposed to know you loved her?" I ask.

"You knew I was moving in on her last night and you still slept with her?" he asks.

"Well, yes but I refuse to feel guilty or ashamed. I shall have you know that we both wanted it, and I first went there before I knew anything about your little infatuation," I say. Not that it would have stopped me.

"It's not an infatuation!" he yells.

"This makes no sense, you were egging us on!" I say incredulously.

"Yeah, but I never thought you'd actually do it!" His eyes then shift past me, and I realise there's a pounding heart nearby. While I am distracted, Nicholas lunges at me and pushes me backwards. I fly through the house and outside. Another door destroyed. Lawrence and Evangeline grab Nicholas's flailing arms and yank him back.

"Why would you do this to me?" he yells at me. He has really lost it. Regaining my senses, I'm in front of him, trying to calm him down. I've never seen Nicholas so enraged before. He's all fangs and ink black eyes. Anger consumes him. Right now Rosannah cannot stay here; I have to get her to leave! I turn to her.

"Get out of here!" I tell her. She just stares at me. She is not going anywhere without her keys, you moron! I shoot off to the study, punch in the code to the safe, grab her bag, and shoot back. I know that unless I show her, I do not want her here, she will not leave. Matching my brother's eyes, I turn on her. I throw the bag at her with a small bit of force, enough to cause her a step back.

"Get the fuck out of here, NOW!" I scream at her. Horror flashes across her face and she flees. We continue to hold a struggling Nicholas as I listen to Rosannah drive away. I am glad I did not get the chance to shut the gate and garage this morning. As she speeds off down the road, my heart is like a stone in my chest weighing me down.

"Nicholas, you've got to snap out of this!" Lawrence pleads. Nicholas lets out a pained cry and crumples to the floor pulling us all down with him.

"Nicholas?" I ask softly.

"I will never forgive you for this," he says looking at me with cold dead black eyes. We all stare at him horrified. He uses this to his advantage and throws us off. He then dashes off and into the entertaining room. 'Smash.' Evangeline follows him.

"He's gone through the French doors!" she yells. Lawrence is in front of me.

"I'll go after him and make sure he doesn't do anything stupid," he says.

"You knew he loved her did you not?" I ask him.

"I didn't think he would go this far," he says.

"Just go and sort him out," I say, and he races off after him. Evangeline comes back as I stand up.

"Don't worry. He's gone off in the opposite direction of Rosannah." She half smiles. Walking off, I ignore her and head to my study. How I will get Rosannah back here? I have well and truly messed this up. I have made a terrible mistake and I may not be able to rectify it.

I do not know how long I have sat here, but I have been in a void. There is nothing but silence. The house is dead without Rosannah. An empty shell. And for the first time in three hundred years, I know what it is like to have a broken heart.

CHAPTER THIRTY-FOUR

Unknown

"There has been a slight hitch," they say as they grovel in front of me.

I already know what this hitch is. I also know it happened days ago, but I enjoy playing games.

"What do you mean there was a hitch? You promised me nothing would go wrong," I growl.

"Raphael came back and found Alex," they say in a quiet voice. Anger boils up inside of me. I worked with them on a recommendation. I had doubts at the time, but they very quickly turned into regret.

"Can you not do anything right? He was supposed to go there when no one would be in for a LONG TIME!" I yell. They shrivel back at the ferocity of my voice. They are terrified of me, but what I have promised keeps them loyal.

"He came back early. I'm not sure why, " they reply. I know why, but I'm not about to explain that. I know it's possible to scare people to death, and I'm having too much fun.

"Now, they won't leave her alone. Do you not understand the severity of the situation? She cannot be allowed to exist. The Synod are a bunch of pussies and the Monstrums are too sentimental for their own good," I say.

"I understand completely," they say in a rush while they bow their head. How can they possibly understand? The entire secrecy of the vampire population is at risk, and it is something that cannot be outed to the entire world. It will not benefit me, and I am not one for things that aren't in my best interest.

"You cannot fail again. I shall direct Alex myself. I have a plan in mind that I'm sure will work," I tell them, pointing to the door, indicating they can vacate my property.

"What are we going to do?" they ask me.

"You have done enough, but I am sure I will need you in the future. You will wait until I next contact you," I say. With a nervous laugh, they leave.

I get out my voice distorter and pick up my mobile phone. I punch in a number and it's answered after two rings. "Hello Alex, I have a new mission for you," I say in a robotic voice.

ABOUT THE AUTHOR

Taniquelle Tulipano is an adult romance author who resides in London, England with her husband and daughter.

For updates and to find out more visit:
www.taniquelletulipano.com
www.facebook.com/taniquelletulipano

BOOKS BY TANIQUELLE TULIPANO

The Monstrum Vampire Series

Dead Beginnings (Monstrum #1)
The Lost Brother (Monstrum #2)
Princess of the Dark (Monstrum #3)

Printed in Great Britain
by Amazon